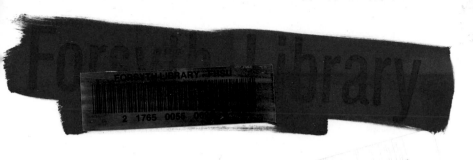

*Nobody Calls*
*at This Hour*
*Just to Say Hello*

By *Irene Kampen*

NOBODY CALLS AT THIS HOUR JUST TO SAY HELLO

ARE YOU CARRYING ANY GOLD
OR LIVING RELATIVES?

DUE TO LACK OF INTEREST
TOMORROW HAS BEEN CANCELED

HERE COMES THE BRIDE,
THERE GOES MOTHER

LAST YEAR AT SUGARBUSH

EUROPE WITHOUT GEORGE

THE ZIEGFELDS' GIRL
(*With Patricia Ziegfeld and Suzanne Gleaves*)

WE THAT ARE LEFT

LIFE WITHOUT GEORGE

# Nobody Calls at This Hour Just to Say Hello

IRENE KAMPEN

DOUBLEDAY & COMPANY, INC.
GARDEN CITY, NEW YORK 1975

For *Joyce* and *Ed*,
a souvenir

*818.5*
*KISM*
*1975*

Library of Congress Cataloging in Publication Data

Kampen, Irene.
   Nobody calls at this hour just to say hello.

   1. Kampen, Irene—Biography. I. Title.
PS3561.A44Z52   818'.5'409 [B]
ISBN 0-385-04566-2
Library of Congress Catalog Card Number 71-175385

# Contents

# Nobody Calls
# at This Hour
# Just to Say Hello

# 1

# Nobody Calls
# at This Hour
# Just to Say Hello

This was my mother:

It is a balmy spring afternoon in Ridgefield, Connecticut, a peaceful town about seventy miles from the din and bustle of New York City.

My father is on the terrace of his home on the banks of the Norwalk River, contemplating the beauties of rural New England.

My mother is pottering around somewhere below, tidying up the riverbank.

"The peace," my father says to himself. He puffs contentedly on his pipe. All is well, he reflects. The tulips are in bloom. The economy is thriving. His two daughters are grown. His wife is happy. "Tranquillity," my father says aloud, and liking the sound of the word he says, again, "tranquillity."

There is an ominous splash from the direction of his ornamental carp pond.

"What now?" my father says.

What now is that two chipmunks have been playfully chasing each other around the pond and one of them has slipped and fallen into the water. It is paddling about in a hopeless circle uttering cries of distress.

"Mary!" my father calls to my mother.

My mother fails to hear him.

"Mary!" he calls again. This time she hears him. The note of panic in his voice is unmistakable.

"I'm coming, Jack," Mother calls, bounding up toward the terrace. "I'm on my way, dear. Stay calm!"

Whatever it is taking place at the carp pond, Mother will handle it. People are always calling "Mary!" or "Mother!" or "Mrs. Trepel!" to her in varying degrees of alarm. "Mother, I've locked myself out of the car again!" they cry, or "Mrs. Trepel, United Parcel in Norwalk. Our driver just found one of your cats under the seat of his truck."

Once the call was "Mary, Cyril here." (Cyril Ritchard, eminent actor, whose home is just across the river.) "I've discovered termites in my baseboards."

If Mother is unable to immediately retrieve the cat or locate the car keys or find an exterminator, Mother can at least give an *at least*.

An *at least* is a "well,-it's-a-terrible-thing-that-has-happened-but-at-least-there-is-one-bright-spot" statement.

In the case of Mr. Ritchard's termites, Mother gave a classic *at least*.

"Well, Cyril," Mother said, "at least the weather is getting warmer and you'll soon be able to sit outside."

Back to the chipmunk:

"What's happened?" Mother demands, arriving breathless at Daddy's side.

"A baby chipmunk fell into the carp pond," my father says. This is a big fat lie. The chipmunk is not a baby, it is a full-grown adult chipmunk and my father is aware of the fact.

My father is also aware that he is dealing here with a woman who, if informed that a baby viper had fallen into a pond would plunge in to rescue it, poisonous fangs and all.

"The baby chipmunk is drowning," Daddy says. "What are we going to do?"

Mother surveys the situation with a lightning glance. "Run up to the attic and bring down your old golf umbrella, dear," she says.

My father stares at her. His old golf umbrella? Has the woman gone mad? Nobody is playing golf. No rain is falling. A chipmunk is drowning, and this woman is calling for old golf umbrellas?

"Hurry, dear," Mother tells him.

Daddy knows better than to argue. If Mother is sending for old golf umbrellas, Mother must have her reasons. He trots off obediently.

"It's in the corner under the eaves behind the old piano bench," Mother calls after him.

How come my mother is not only ready without a moment's hesitation to demand old golf umbrellas for the rescue of drowning chipmunks, but she also knows exactly where old golf umbrellas are stored?

Because, like the Boy Scouts, Mother is prepared.

"The thoughts of others," the poet Housman wrote,
"Were light and fleeting
"Of lovers' meeting, or luck or fame.
"Mine were of trouble and mine were steady
"So I was ready
"When trouble came."

Mother went through life expecting the worst. If her telephone rang after eight o'clock at night it was going to bring bad news, according to Mother, and the bad news was probably going to involve one of her children.

"What's the matter?" Mother would demand. "What's wrong? Why are you calling so late?" (8:45 P.M.) "I can tell by your voice that something is bothering you. What is it?"

It was impossible to convince her that you had merely telephoned to say hello. "Nobody calls at this hour just to say hello," Mother would say suspiciously.

> *Transcript of a long-distance telephone conversation between a Jewish mother in Connecticut and her daughter who is away on a trip to Cleveland, Ohio*

MOTHER: Irene? What's wrong?

DAUGHTER: Nothing is wrong, Mother. I felt like saying hello to you.

MOTHER: Something has happened out there in Cleveland. Tell me what it is.

DAUGHTER: Everything is fine. Nothing has happened.

MOTHER: I can tell by the sound of your voice that something is wrong.

DAUGHTER: Nothing is wrong! Everything is marvelous! How are you, Mother? How are the cats?

MOTHER: Nellie hasn't eaten a morsel for three days, poor darling. Now tell me—what has gone wrong? Do you need money?

DAUGHTER: I have money. I have cash. I have traveler's checks. I have my bankbook. I have credit cards.

MOTHER: I don't want you out there in Cleveland with things going wrong and no money in your purse.

DAUGHTER: Mother!

MOTHER: (*Subsiding*) Well, you sound to me as though you're coming down with a cold.

I'm sorry to say that usually Mother was right, too—I was either coming down with a cold or else something had gone wrong out in Cleveland. Occasionally, both.

"Mark my words, that ornamental carp pond will someday be a death trap," Chicken Little, played by Mary Trepel, had warned five years before. Daddy had just announced his plans to have such a pond constructed next to the terrace.

"This pond," Daddy said, "will be twelve inches deep at its deepest point. For whom will it be a death trap, may I inquire?"

"Never mind," Mother said. Whenever Mother said "Never mind" in a particular tone of voice you could be 99 per cent positive that whatever she was never-minding about was going to turn out to be true.

"I warned him it would be a death trap," Mother says now, waiting at the pool for Daddy to return with the umbrella. "Every minute of these five years I've been expecting something like this to happen and now it has."

Daddy returns with the old golf umbrella. "Give it here, dear," Mother says. She unfurls the umbrella, kneels at the side of the pool, and scoops the chipmunk, along with half a dozen unlucky carp, out of the pond with it.

"Everything will be all right," Mother assures Daddy. She carries the umbrella full of carp and chipmunk into the kitchen. She lights the oven, wraps the chipmunk in an old bath towel, and fills the sink with water.

She dumps the carp into the sink, forces a teaspoonful of brandy down the chipmunk's throat, and gently places the towel-wrapped chipmunk into the warm oven to recover.

Poor darling Nellie, Mother's cat, wanders into the

kitchen. Nellie has scented the aroma of roasting brandied chipmunk wafting through the house.

"You're starved, aren't you, poor darling?" Mother says, petting Nellie and giving her a handful of Cat Yummies. Mother is now in her element. She is at one and the same time sheltering carp, feeding a starving cat, and being a Jewish mother to a sick chipmunk.

Being a Jewish mother to a sick chipmunk has a great advantage over being a Jewish mother to a sick daughter. A sick chipmunk is not apt to turn peevish and say, "I'm all *right*, Mother. Don't fuss so. I feel perfectly well and I don't want to lie in the oven wrapped in an old bath towel. Mother, *please!*"

The chipmunk begins to make feeble recovery sounds. "Feeling better, are we?" Mother says. She removes it from the oven and carries it outside to a sunny spot on the lawn.

"Back to your pond, poor fellows," Mother tells the carp, scooping them into a bucket and dumping them into the pond once more. She scours out the sink.

"We're starved, aren't we?" she inquires of my former Siamese cat, The Prince. Several years earlier Mother had adopted The Prince after rescuing him from what she considered an unsuitable home (mine). "Here's a little snack for you and poor darling Nellie," Mother tells The Prince, setting out on the floor a cat smorgasbord of canned mackerel, condensed milk, boiled shrimp, and some more Yummies.

"Just in time for *The Secret Storm*," Mother says, glancing at the kitchen clock. She settles down in the living room to watch today's episode of her favorite soap opera.

"I think I can explain to you gentlemen on the hospital board the reasons for Nurse Penny's peculiar behavior in the operating room," Dr. Matthews, chief neurological surgeon of Rosehill Hospital is saying, when there is an ominous splash from the direction of the ornamental carp pond.

"Mary!" my father shouts.

"Damn it," Mother says. She turns the TV set off and leans out the window. "What is it, Jack dear?" she calls.

"A baby chipmunk has fallen into the carp pond," Daddy says.

"Is it the same baby chipmunk that fell into the carp pond an hour ago?" Mother asks.

"I'm pretty sure it is," Daddy says.

"In that case, the hell with it, dear," Mother says, going back to *The Secret Storm*. Enough, Mother feels, is enough.

## GLOSSARY

| *Statement by Mother* | *Actual Reality* |
| --- | --- |
| **CATS** | |
| Haven't eaten a morsel of food for three days. | Have eaten one pound shrimp, three jars Beech Nut Baby Food, one carton Cat Yummies, one-half can mackerel, one robin. |
| Haven't been home all night. Probably run over and killed on the road. | Sleeping in garage. |
| Saw me packing my suitcase for a trip and crawled away brokenhearted to hide under the bed. | Sleeping under bed. |
| Haven't been home for forty-eight hours. Never stayed away this long before. Probably drowned in Norwalk River. | Sleeping someplace. |

## GLOSSARY (*Continued*)

### GRANDCHILDREN

*Christine* (My daughter) Awarded highest degree ever granted in America in biochemistry or is it biology? Engaged in secret research, always wears white smock, is on threshold of winning Nobel prize, compares favorably with Madame Curie.

Has Ph.D. in Genetics.

*Susie* (My sister's daughter) Most beautiful, gentlenatured, finest bone structure, longest hair, thickest lashes, sweetest smile, attends finest college in America, talented enough to go on stage and make a fortune playing guitar, compares favorably with Andrés Segovia.

Antioch student. Plays guitar.

*Tommy* (My sister's son) Highest IQ ever recorded in America, speaks several languages, has amazed pedagogical circles with his grasp of mathematics, sings, dances, writes, composes brilliantly, compares favorably with the young Leonardo da Vinci.

Sixteen years old. Taking driving lessons.

"He's heartbroken," Mother tells me. 'He' is The Prince. "He's been moping all afternoon. He senses that I'm leaving him to spend the weekend at Uncle Wolfram's."

"Cats are not capable of human emotions," I tell her. "Their hearts do not break. They do not mope. They do not know Uncle Wolfram from a trumpeter swan."

The Prince puts on his Yiddish Art Theater act, baring his teeth at me like Morris Carnovsky playing King Lear.

"Never mind," Mother tells me. "Tomorrow is Columbus Day. Christopher Columbus was Jewish." Mother specializes in who famous is Jewish.

"Christopher Columbus?" I say. "Oh, Mother!"

"Never mind," Mother says. She lights her twenty-seventh cigarette of the day and says, "I'll tell you who else is Jewish. Richard Burton, that's who."

"Oh, *Mother!*" I say.

"Never mind," Mother says. "Mark my words."

"Richard Burton is not Jewish," I tell her patiently. "Richard Burton is Welsh. He was born in Wales of Welsh parents. He grew up in Wales. He went to school in Wales. His father was a Welsh coal miner."

"Never mind," Mother says again. "I happen to know."*

I say later to my sister, Joyce, "Guess who's Jewish now? Christopher Columbus and Richard Burton!"

We both have a good laugh over this, but the next day Joyce tells me she looked Christopher Columbus up in the Encyclopaedia Britannica, just for her own amusement. "He was Jewish," Joyce says.

There is a silence. What can we say? "At least," I tell Joyce, "give me an at least."

Joyce thinks about it for a moment. "At least Mother isn't going around claiming that the Queen of England is Jewish," she says.

I repeat Joyce's remark to Mother. Mother says, "Never mind, with that nose of hers it wouldn't surprise me at all."

---

* Mother was right. Richard Burton is Jewish. Part Jewish, anyway. Jewish grandmother.

# 2

# *And They Lived Happily Ever After*

Daddy and Mother met when Mother was eighteen years old.

"When I met your father he was a dapper man about Brooklyn who owned a chain of retail flower shops," Mother told me. "He was very handsome. He wore spats and a straw hat. He danced like a dream. He had beautiful manners."

He also had a fiancée, but the moment he laid eyes on the lovely young Mary Harris it was all over.

"I had just arrived from Houston, Texas," Mother said. "I was introduced to Daddy at a cousin's house somewhere in Brooklyn. He asked if he could take me dancing the following night."

I have a photograph of Mother taken at the time. She was slim as a wand. Her eyes were emerald green and her skin was flawless. She had an enchanting smile.

"Daddy proposed to me two weeks after we met," Mother said. "We were dancing the waltz on the old revolving floor of Riesenweber's at the time. He took the diamond engagement ring out of his pocket and put it on my finger right there on the dance floor."

The next day he sent her a dozen American Beauty roses and a dozen pairs of white kid opera gloves. They were married in the parlor of Aunt Anna's house and they went to Atlantic City on their honeymoon.

"You were born a year later," Mother told me. "We named you Irene after the heroine of the musical comedy *Irene* which had just opened on Broadway. Daddy had been enchanted by the heroine of that name."

I was a sickly baby. When I was about three months old I developed some mysterious malady that the doctors were unable to diagnose.

"You lay in your crib wailing and burning with fever," Mother told me. "The doctors finally told us that there was no hope. You were too ill. You were going to die."

At that point, according to Mother, Grandma Trepel came into my nursery and without a word went to the closet and got my pink silk baby bonnet. Then she vanished.

"She was gone all day," Mother said. "You got sicker and sicker. Grandma got back to the house that evening. She came into the nursery where Daddy and I were standing over your crib, weeping, and she said to us, 'Stop crying. Irene will get well.'"

The next morning my fever had disappeared. I had recovered completely.

And where had Grandma Trepel vanished with my pink silk baby bonnet?

"She had taken a taxicab to Delancey Street on New York's lower East Side," Mother said. "She went up and down Delancey Street asking questions of all the shopkeepers and passers-by until she found the answer she had been seeking."

The answer led her to the basement apartment of an old man—a poor Jewish immigrant known as *Tsadaka Yid,* which translated means *pious Jew.*

"Grandma described your symptoms to the old man," Mother went on. "He took your bonnet and said a prayer over it. Then he told Grandma to return home. 'The evil spirits have been driven from the baby,' he told Grandma. 'Your granddaughter will get well now.'"

Grandma came home and waited. In the morning I was well.

"And from that moment on you never had a sick day," Mother told me, "and Grandma Trepel herself lived to be ninety-six and died peacefully in her sleep, God rest her good soul."

It is my favorite family story. The moral is that you don't have to be Jewish to be exorcised of the devil, but it helps.

My sister, Joyce, was born when I was eight years old.

"Why 'Joyce'?" I said to my parents. I wasn't too thrilled at the idea of sharing the spotlight with a brand-new baby sister in the first place, and in the second place I didn't think the name "Joyce" was fancy enough to be paired with Irene, the heroine of a Broadway musical comedy.

"Because Joyce is a pretty name," my parents told me, "and she fills us with joy by being here."

"I think you ought to call her Pamela," I said. "Her nickname could be Pammy. Pammy Trepel sounds cuter than plain old Joyce Trepel."

"Her name is Joyce," my mother said, "and I don't want to hear any more about it."

"Pammy," I said rebelliously, and from then on and for a

long time whenever Mother and Daddy were out of ear-shot I called Joyce, Pammy.

"Smile at big sister, Pammy," I would coax Pammy-Joyce as she lay in her carriage. "Wave bye-bye to the lady, Pammy."

I also spread abroad throughout the neighborhood the rumor that Pammy-Joyce wasn't my real sister at all, but had been adopted by my parents from a poor family who lived on a houseboat in Sheepshead Bay.

"I'm the one who told Mother and Daddy about the poor little newborn baby that had to eat garbage and had no milk to drink because her family was on relief," I reported piously to anyone who would listen. "If it hadn't been for me the baby's parents would have thrown it away, probably."

"Do you mean to say that Joyce isn't your sister at all?" my listener would say in fascination.

"Her name isn't really Joyce," I would say. "It's actually Pamela. Pammy for short. My parents changed it to Joyce so her real parents would never be able to find her again."

Mother was understandably furious with me when she heard news of this tale I was spreading. Pammy-Joyce, of course, was too young to care.

"It was a cruel and silly story to tell people about your innocent baby sister," Mother said to me. "How could you be so wicked?"

"I'm sure Irene didn't mean to be wicked," Daddy said. "She probably began to make up a story in her imagination and forgot the difference between what was real and what wasn't."

Daddy could always find something good to say about everybody, even Hitler. ("He must have had an unhappy childhood to have turned out so terribly.")

"Irene would never deliberately do anything bad,"

Daddy said. "Irene is a good sweet child. I'm sure she loves her baby sister, Joyce."

"Pammy," I said under my breath. Fortunately Daddy didn't hear me. Daddy adored both his daughters and nothing could shake his belief that Joyce and I were perfect.

"Your father was a saint," people who knew him still tell me, all these long years since he has been gone. He was a saint and, like all good saints, he had a few tiny faults.

He had the world's worst sense of direction. He inherited this from his father, Grandpa Trepel, who fled the pogroms in Russia to escape to America. He escaped all right, along with his wife and seven children, but he got muddled up buying the steamship tickets in England and ended up in South America by mistake.

The family had to get back on the boat again and sail back to England. There they got on another boat—headed in the right direction this time—and finally arrived on the right part of the continent.

Daddy didn't ever manage to get lost on the grand scale of his father. Daddy already *was* in America. He did, though, manage to get lost a lot inside the United States, often between his home and the village of Ridgefield itself, a distance of less than four miles.

He got a lot of other people lost too. He had a habit of giving the wrong directions in a right-sounding manner.

"Take a sharp left at the intersection," Daddy would say, meanwhile jotting down the wrong directions on a piece of paper. Sometimes he also dashed off a wrong map on the back of the paper at the same time. "Proceed a tenth of a mile until you come to a traffic light. Bear right. You can't miss it."

Ha!

Daddy also told old jokes wrong.

"Have you heard the joke about the seafood restaurant?" he would ask.

Useless to reply, "Yes, Daddy dear, we've heard it," because he was going to tell it anyway.

"A customer went into this seafood restaurant," Daddy said, "and sat down at a table and said to the waiter, 'Waiter, do you serve clams here?' and the waiter said, 'Certainly, sir. What can I bring you?'"

Daddy waited with an expectant smile. Dead silence.

"Don't you get it?" Daddy said. "The man says 'Do you serve clams here?' and the waiter says 'Yes, what can I bring you?'"

"Crabs, Jack dear," Mother told him with long-suffering forbearance. "It's supposed to be 'Waiter, do you serve *crabs* here.' It isn't funny if the customer asks for clams. It doesn't make any sense if he asks for clams. There's no point to the story if he asks for clams. *Crabs!* 'Do you serve *crabs* here?'"

"I meant to say crabs," Daddy said.

A day or two later he would say, "Have I told you the one about the seafood restaurant? It seems that this customer went in and said, 'Waiter, do you serve clams here?'"

Daddy suffered a severe heart attack when he was over seventy. "He won't recover," the doctors told Mother, but he not only recovered, he went back to work commuting to his flower shops in New York three days a week. He also invented some marvelous new magic tricks. He supervised the construction on his Ridgefield property of a flagstone terrace and an ornamental carp pond.

"Every time I look down the driveway and see a truck drive up carrying two Italian laborers and a cement mixer," Mother said, "I know it's going to cost us another five hundred dollars, minimum."

Daddy also took up a new hobby—oil painting.

"Call me Grandpa Moses," he told us. He turned out a never-ending series of sunny landscapes and still-life paintings. He specialized in cows. Mother was critical.

"There's something wrong with your cows, dear," she told him. Daddy demanded to know what was wrong with his cows. "They seem to have too much personality," Mother said. "They don't look like cows as far as their expressions go. They look like people."

Mother was mistaken. I have a painting of Daddy's hanging over my desk—a landscape with a herd of cows in the foreground. The cows look like cows. One or two, I admit, have fairly apprehensive expressions on their faces, and another appears to be smiling at a rock, but on the whole they are more like cows than like people.

Daddy kept on painting until he died at the age of seventy-eight, God rest his good soul. Now there is nobody left who thinks my sister and I are perfect.

How would Mother react to widowhood? Joyce and I were worried. Since the day she and Daddy had been married when she was only eighteen she had never been alone. How would she manage?

Mother mourned for a while, sitting sad and still in her empty house. Then one day she woke up and said, "What can I have been thinking of, those windowpanes are filthy, I must wash them immediately; the dust is an inch thick on the mantel, and look outside at the lawn—it's a disgrace; where is that rat Maynard, the gardener?"

So life began again.

After Daddy died, Mother took up a new hobby—world travel. She and Cousin Barbara began taking an annual trip abroad every summer. There was a lot of high-class talk about museums and the Acropolis by moonlight, but they really went abroad to shop.

Each of them denied this and accused the other.

"I only brought these mantillas back from Spain because your cousin Barbara insisted on spending every minute shopping," Mother told me. "I was longing to go to the Prado and look at the El Grecos, but I couldn't very well go off and leave Barbara alone."

"Your mother refused to do any sightseeing whatsoever in Japan," Cousin Barbara told me. "Not even one single Buddhist shrine did we visit in Kyoto. I couldn't budge her out of the bazaars and I couldn't desert her and go off by myself. You like the kimono? I picked it up in a little shop off the Ginza."

Mother and Cousin Barbara also spent a lot of time abroad in cleaning. They cleaned whatever was at hand at the moment—foreign hotel rooms, Pan-American jets, Dutch cruise ships, Greek ruins—it made no never mind to them.

"I've never been so mortified," Cousin Barbara told me. "We had touched down at Amsterdam. The cleaning crew came swarming through the cabin the way they do and I looked up and there was your mother, Irene, swarming right along with them, emptying ashtrays and tidying up the cabin."

"And who was it sneaked back to the stateroom aboard the *Rotterdam* every morning to make the beds before the Indonesian cabin stewards got there?" Mother inquired indignantly. "Who was it who was always hanging around the ship's laundry room ironing, pray tell?"

"At least I never took a tissue out of my purse in Greece and dusted a pagan altar with it," Cousin Barbara said.

The Bobbsey Twins Abroad were so busy dusting and shopping that they once in a while got mixed up and accidentally toured the same foreign country twice without planning to.

"Why did you go to Morocco again this year, Mother?" my sister, Joyce, inquired. Mother was unpacking her suitcases. "You and Cousin Barbara were in Morocco three summers ago."

"Don't be so silly, Joyce," Mother said. "I'd certainly be aware of it if I had been to Morocco twice."

"Joyce is right, Mother," I said. "Three summers ago was when you brought back that goatskin wallet from Morocco for Uncle Wolfram that he threw away."

"He said it smelled terrible," Joyce reminded Mother. "He said everything that tourists bring back from Morocco smells terrible. He said it's because the Moroccans cure everything in camel pee."

"Was that wallet from Morocco?" Mother said. "Well, it's the last gift I ever bring home from abroad for your uncle Wolfram, mark my words. American Express has a nerve sending us to the same country twice."

American Express handled the annual travel arrangements.

"American Express doesn't know where to send us this summer," Mother said. I said how about Hawaii? "Cousin Barbara doesn't want to go where there's a lot of sand," Mother said.

"Nepal would be exciting to go to," Joyce suggested.

Mother said Cousin Barbara didn't want to go anyplace where there were a lot of mountains.

I proposed a photographic safari out of Nairobi, Africa.

"Cousin Barbara doesn't want to go anyplace where there are a lot of African animals," Mother said. "I, personally, would love to go to Hawaii or Nepal or Nairobi, but you know how your cousin Barbara is when she gets her mind set against something."

"*I'm* perfectly willing to go wherever your mother wants to go," Cousin Barbara told me. "She's the one who refuses to change her mind about anything."

The truth, of course, was that neither Cousin Barbara nor Mother wanted to go to Hawaii or Nepal or Nairobi because the shopping was no good.

"We've decided on Japan," Mother told me.

"I want you to promise me one thing before you go," I said. "I want you to promise not to bring back a lot of gifts for me. I mean it."

"Very well," Mother said, hurt. "If you want to deprive a mother of the pleasure of bringing a gift home to her daughter I certainly won't buy you a thing."

"*One* gift, then," I said. "It's positively ridiculous for you and Cousin Barbara to spend all your time abroad in shopping. I want one gift, thank you in advance, and I'll tell you what I want—I want a lacquered Japanese fan."

Mother brightened. "One fan, remember!" I said.

You know what I got? I got a lacquered Japanese fan, a set of wind chimes, a pair of chopsticks, a pearl ring, a kimono, a miniature camera, a collapsible paper lantern, and a pair of woven rush Japanese sandals.

I also got a carved ivory Buddha, a mother-of-pearl compact, a view of Mt. Fuji in watercolor, a Japanese hibachi, and a set of bamboo place mats.

At least I didn't get a likeness of a Japanese cat made out of thousands and thousands of tiny hand-painted Japanese pebbles.

Pammy-Joyce got that.

# 3

# *Talking About Money Is Vulgar*

"I want you to look at the first item on this menu," Mother said to Daddy. Daddy looked. The first item was "Liver Paté ($1)." "Liver Paté!" Mother said. "Plain ordinary chopped chicken liver that I have two perfectly good jars full of back home in the refrigerator right this minute. One dollar indeed!"

This was Mother in a restaurant—any restaurant.

"And I hope you notice that they're charging one dollar for a bowl of borscht," Mother went on, pursuing her hobby of reading the right side of the menu when taken out to dine. "My grandmother Goldstein, may she rest in peace, would turn in her grave if she could see them charging a dollar for a bowl of borscht."

"The waiter is here, dear," Daddy said.

"It's nothing but cabbage soup," Mother said. "The poorest peasants in Russia ate borscht every day of their lives."

"How about some Little Neck clams on the half shell to

start with?" Daddy said to Mother. Mother wasn't through with the borscht situation yet.

"A few pennies' worth of ingredients are all that are needed to make a whole enormous kettle of borscht," Mother said. "Two kettles, possibly."

"The filet mignon sounds good," Daddy said. "Or perhaps a Chateaubriand for two. What do you think, dear?"

"Nobody could *lift* a dollar's worth of borscht," Mother said.

"We'll have the filet mignon," Daddy told the waiter, but Mother said, "You have the filet mignon, dear, I'll take the fillet of flounder."

Fillet of flounder was the cheapest item on the menu.

"Oh, come on, have the filet mignon," Daddy urged her. "Or maybe you'd like the roast prime ribs of beef?"

"No thank you, dear," Mother said. "Fillet of flounder will be just fine—although they have some nerve to charge five dollars when it was on sale this very morning in the A and P—" But at Daddy's look, she subsided. "Fillet of flounder please," she told the waiter.

Daddy was a big spender and a lavish tipper. Mother's in-depth cost analyses of the menu irritated him and he told her so, over and over, but it didn't stop Mother.

"There's no sense ordering dessert," Mother would say, "when I have a lovely chocolate pie at home just sitting in the icebox."

Mother's battle against the cost of dining out was never ending, but futile because Joyce and I happily followed Daddy's menu suggestions whenever the family ate together in a restaurant.

"We'd like the Chateaubriand for two, please, with fresh asparagus on the side and salad with Roquefort dressing," Joyce would tell the waiter. Roquefort dressing was fifty cents extra. "And shrimp cocktail first," Joyce said.

Shrimp cocktail was a dollar extra. Mother could hardly bear it.

"And I'll have Cherries Jubilee for dessert," I told the waiter.

Seventy-five cents extra. Mother sighed audibly. Daddy frowned at her. The waiter said, "Will madame have any dessert?"

Madame said no indeed, there was a perfectly good choc—

"Mary!" Daddy said.

"No, thank you, no dessert," Mother said.

Mother had grown up as a poor girl in a poor family and she never was able to get over feeling poor, hard as Daddy tried to convince her that there was enough money in the bank to cover the cost of the Cherries Jubilee and the Chateaubriand.

For their anniversary Daddy bought her a diamond bracelet and a diamond ring. "And I want you to wear them," Daddy told her sternly. "I don't want you to put them away in the vault because you think they're too good to wear."

Mother promised to wear the diamonds, and she did. She also used the same scouring pad over and over and over until it was a rusty scrap to clean the pots with while she was wearing the diamonds.

"Why are you throwing out that perfectly good scouring pad?" Mother asked me, eying my garbage can with a disapproving eye.

"Because I've used it," I said. "It's all rusty. It's disgusting-looking."

"It's a perfectly good scouring pad," Mother said, snatching it out of the garbage can. "I can use it to clean the bottom of the ornamental carp pond. And why are you throwing away this perfectly good flannel nightgown?"

"It's torn," I said. "There's a big rip in the hem."

"I can use it as a dustcloth," Mother said. She went back home with my perfectly good scouring pad and my perfectly good flannel nightgown. She didn't clean out the carp pond or dust with them either. She scoured a pot with one and wore the other to bed.

"What is that you've got on, Mother?" I would ask her in despair. Mother said it was my old woolen skirt that I had given her last winter.

"You said you were going to make a hooked rug out of it," I said.

"It's still perfectly good," Mother said. Mother was of the opinion that I spent my money like a drunken sailor, although it was hard to picture a drunken sailor squandering his pay on new scouring pads and flannel nightgowns while at the same time tossing away perfectly good woolen skirts. "This skirt is fine for me to wear around the house," Mother said. "Nothing wrong with it at all."

Mother had a closet full of expensive dresses which she would wear if absolutely forced to at gunpoint. "It's much too good to wear," was her refrain. "I'll save it for some special occasion."

Then she would put on one of my perfectly good old skirts and one of Joyce's perfectly good discarded sweaters that the moths had eaten and she would get into the car and drive all over the state of Connecticut looking for a sale on roasting chickens.

"Thirty-two cents a pound!" she would exclaim happily, pouncing on the bargain chicken to take it home, roast it, stuff it, chop up its liver, make chicken soup out of what was left, and serve the entire repast for dinner.

"If you ordered this meal in a restaurant it would cost at least ten dollars per person," she would announce.

If Uncle Ingomar happened to be present at the table a

wintry smile would pass across his face at the thought of
how much money he and Aunt Anna were not spending by
having dinner at our house and eating Mother's free ten-
dollar chicken dinner.

Uncle Ingomar was a millionaire. "He's Aunt Anna's second husband," Mother explained to Joyce and me. "You
children must never talk about Aunt Anna's first husband
in front of Uncle Ingomar."

First husband had done something disgraceful and afterward vanished, leaving Aunt Anna deserted and penniless.
Joyce and I could never find out exactly what the something disgraceful had been.

"Never mind, it was terrible," Mother said. "Aunt Anna
never got over it."

"Self-exposure on the subway," Joyce guessed.

"Much worse," Mother said. "We won't discuss it any
longer, if you don't mind. And remember what I warned
you about—never mention him in front of Uncle Ingomar."

Joyce and I were forbidden to mention President Roosevelt in front of Uncle Ingomar either. Uncle Ingomar
believed in his heart that President Roosevelt was plotting
to take all Uncle Ingomar's money away and distribute it to
a lot of poor people.

"Particularly those damn Puerto Ricans," Uncle Ingomar said.

Mother also told us not to talk about money in front of
Aunt Anna and Uncle Ingomar either. "They're rich,"
Mother explained. "They consider it vulgar to discuss
money."

"If I were rich I'd talk about my money," Joyce said. "I'd
talk about it all the time."

"We aren't allowed to talk about first husband in front of
Uncle Ingomar," I complained, "and we aren't allowed to

talk about money and we aren't allowed to talk about President Roosevelt. What's left to talk to him about?"

Mother said, "Talk to him about his hobby."

Uncle Ingomar's hobby was collecting matchbook covers, possibly because matchbook covers were free and cost nothing to collect, unlike Chinese jade or French Impressionists. "Your uncle Ingomar has one of the largest collections of matchbook covers in the United States," Mother said.

Uncle Ingomar's other hobby was never spending any money whatsoever if possible.

"In my entire life," he once informed me proudly, "I have ridden in a taxicab only twice."

My immediate reaction to this was to go downtown and buy myself a giant-size carton of brand-new scouring pads.

Aunt Anna's hobby was changing her last will and testament.

"Are you in or out?" was a common question among members of the family. I had been in from my day of birth because Daddy was Aunt Anna's favorite brother. On my fourth birthday, before Mother had a chance to stop me, I am told that I said to Aunt Anna, "What did your first husband do that was so bad, Auntie Anna? Did he go to jail for it?"

Aunt Anna rushed home and summoned her attorneys and threw me out. I was in and out a number of times over the years. When Aunt Anna died I was in, and very grateful I am to her indeed.

"Who do you suppose they'll leave the bulk of their money to?" was another common question among members of the family.

Aunt Anna and Uncle Ingomar had no children of their own. Before World War II, late in the nineteen-thirties, they suddenly adopted, sight unseen, a German orphan named Franz. Franz was shipped over to the United States by boat.

"They're adopting the kid purely out of spite," Uncle Wolfram said. Uncle Wolfram was out at the moment. "They'll put this Franz in and throw the rest of the family out, mark my words."

According to Aunt Anna and Uncle Ingomar, Franz was a chubby golden-haired toddler just learning to talk. "The Berlin adoption agency wrote us a complete description of him," Aunt Anna said. "He sounds adorable. Uncle Ingomar and I have redecorated the billiard room as a nursery. We can hardly wait to see little Franz."

There must have been some misunderstanding between the Berlin adoption agency and Aunt Anna and Uncle Ingomar because Franz upon his arrival aboard the *Bremen* turned out to be a pudgy adolescent with a permanent scowl and a habit of clicking his heels and shouting "Bitte!" He was hastily unadopted and shipped back to the Fatherland. We later heard that he joined Hitler's Youth Corps.

"And I have been put back in again," Uncle Wolfram told Mother. "Anna herself assured me."

Aunt Anna and Uncle Ingomar died when they both were in their eighties. The last will and testament was read aloud to the assembled relatives in the offices of Murratrow, Henneman and Wirtz, attorneys at law.

Item One consisted of a number of monetary bequests to the lucky ins. Item Two was a provision for the sale of some property.

" 'Item Three,' " the attorney read. " 'My collection of matchbook covers I do devise and bequeath intact to my beloved relative Wolfram Trepel. Item Four: stocks and bonds currently in possession of custody department of Chase Manhattan Bank—' "

"Just one moment," Uncle Wolfram said. The attorney looked up from the document. "Are you giving me to understand that I have inherited Uncle Ingomar's matchbook cover collection?" Uncle Wolfram asked.

"Indeed you have," the attorney said. "And may I offer my congratulations, sir? A fine collection, I am given to understand."

"That's all I'm getting?" Uncle Wolfram said incredulously. "No money? Not even a pair of cuff links? Just matchbooks?"

"It is quite an extensive collection, sir," the attorney said. "One of the largest in the United States, I believe. It contains well over three thousand specimens, give or take a few hundred."

Uncle Wolfram stood up and told Murratrow, Henneman and Wirtz what they could do with their three thousand specimens. He stormed out of the office.

"We'll continue with the reading of the will now," the attorney said. He cleared his throat. "The remainder of the document deals with the bulk of the estate and is couched in extremely difficult technical language. With your permission I will present it to you in simple everyday English."

He cleared his throat again and said, "In simple everyday English, the bulk of the estate has been bequeathed to the Carmelita Home for Aged and Indigent."

There was a deafening silence.

"The who?" Mother said faintly, at last.

"The Carmelita Home for Aged and Indigent," the attorney said. "It is a charitable institution located, I believe, up in Spanish Harlem."

"How much money is in the bulk of the estate?" Joyce asked, probably figuring that it was okay to talk about

Uncle Ingomar's money without being considered vulgar now that Uncle Ingomar was gone.

"Over one million dollars," the attorney said. "Give or take a few thousand."

"Would you be good enough to repeat," Aunt Trauba, Uncle Wolfram's wife, said to the attorney, "the name of the establishment which is going to inherit this one million dollars? Once more, if you will be so kind?"

The attorney said, slowly and clearly, "The Carmelita Home for Aged and Indigent."

"I see," Aunt Trauba said, although none of us did, really. Uncle Ingomar had all his life been opposed to giving anything, even a matchbook cover, away for free to anybody either aged or indigent, particularly anybody up in Spanish Harlem.

"Well, at least," Mother said, "at least . . . at least . . ."
But for once there were no at leasts.

The Carmelita Home wrote Mother a letter asking for a photograph of Aunt Anna and Uncle Ingomar to hang in the lounge so the aged and indigent could see what their benefactors looked like.

"I'm certainly not going to go out and spend good money to have a photograph enlarged and framed for the Carmelita Home," Mother said. "What a nerve!"

She went up to the attic and rummaged around in a box full of old Christmas cards until she found one that Aunt Anna and Uncle Ingomar had sent with a photograph of themselves on it. She put the card into an envelope and mailed it off to the Carmelita Home, postage due. "There!" she said.

Uncle Ingomar would have approved heartily.

# 4

# *Blossom*

"Tell me if I'm imagining this," my sister, Joyce, says. "I'm a tiny child and I'm sitting on somebody's lap in a rose garden except it isn't a rose garden, it's a basement. But it's also a German saloon—"

"Except it isn't a saloon, it's a theater," I say.

"How did you know?" Joyce says. "There's a man on the stage dressed like a devil in red satin complete with horns and a tail. He's carrying a dagger—no, no, the whole thing is too silly. I must have dreamed it."

"You didn't dream it and you didn't imagine it," I say. "It was one of Mother and Daddy's big magic parties and you were allowed to stay up late and watch the tricks. The devil was Uncle Wolfram Trepel, who always billed himself as the 'Marvelous Mephisto.'"

Daddy's lifelong avocation was magic, Mother was his onstage assistant, and most of their friends were magicians, both amateur and professional.

The rose garden was the basement of our house in Brooklyn. The original owners of the house had decorated the cellar as a rose garden with red and pink climbing paper roses all over the walls. The whole place was bathed in fake moonlight.

When Mother and Daddy bought the house they not only kept the rose garden; they added a small stage and also an authentic German saloon. The saloon was transported piecemeal from some auction house in St. Louis and painstakingly reconstructed in the Brooklyn basement, complete with swinging doors, a brass footrail, and a stuffed bluefish mounted over the mirror.

"Mother and Daddy gave a gala magic party to celebrate the redecoration of the cellar," I told Joyce. "Most of the famous magicians of the day came—Blackstone, and Thurston, and Cardini—but that didn't stop Uncle Wolfram from getting up on stage after all of them had performed and trying to do his dagger-through-the-card trick."

"You are completely satisfied," Uncle Wolfram's patter ran (patter is the vocal monologue with which a magician accompanies his tricks) "that there is no possibility whatsoever that I could know which card has been secretly chosen?"

No possibility whatsoever.

"In that case I now stab the sealed deck with my dagger and—Abracadabra!—the card impaled on the tip of the dagger is the very card that was secretly chosen—the two of clubs!"

Unfortunately, the secret card was the queen of diamonds.

"Darn it anyway," Uncle Wolfram would say crossly, twitching his red satin tail. "I'll try the trick again—heck, it's bound to work *some*time. Watch closely now, because the closer you watch, the less you see. The hand is quicker than the eye. Hocus-Pocus!"

But whether Uncle Wolfram said "Hocus-Pocus!" or

"Abracadabra!" or "Sim-Sala-Bim!" it never made much difference; the dagger ended up sticking through the wrong card anyway.

"Darn!" Uncle Wolfram said again. The audience stirred restively. "The heck with it," Uncle Wolfram said, discarding his dagger and his sealed deck. "I shall now demonstrate for you the amazing hypnotic powers of Marvelous Mephisto."

He turned to Mother. "Kindly get Blossom down here," he told her. "I want to put her under."

Blossom was our maid.

"Blossom is upstairs in the kitchen making potato salad, Wolfram," Mother said.

"The potato salad must wait," Uncle Wolfram said. "The show must go on."

Blossom was Uncle Wolfram's favorite hypnotic subject. She was very flashy-looking, with jet-black hair piled in a nest of curls on top of her head and anchored with a fake gardenia which glowed in the dark. She also always wore spike-heeled ankle-strap pumps, even when making potato salad in our kitchen.

"Blossom!" Mother called. "Come downstairs and be hypnotized."

Blossom came downstairs, slave bracelets jangling.

"Sit right here onstage, my dear," Marvelous Mephisto told her. Blossom sat down, giggling. "I stand behind you and place my hands on your shoulders, thus," Marvelous Mephisto said. "You will now close your eyes." Blossom closed her eyes.

"You are growing drowsy," Marvelous Mephisto told Blossom. "You are relaxed—you are almost asleep—" Blossom's head nodded. It didn't take much to put Blossom under.

"You are asleep," Mephisto said. Blossom snored once.

"When I clap my hands together," Mephisto said, "you will awaken. You will feel completely normal except for the fact that you will believe yourself to be a chicken."

Mephisto clapped his hands together sharply.

"Cluck," Blossom said, opening her eyes. "Cluck. Squawk." She flapped her elbows. "Cluck," she said again.

"You will remain a chicken until I snap my fingers thrice," Mephisto said.

"Cluck," Blossom said. "Squawk."

Everybody applauded. Uncle Wolfram bowed. "Wolfram is really getting quite professional," Aunt Trauba said proudly. The show was over. The guests stood up and began to move about.

"You'd better get back to the kitchen and finish making your potato salad," Mother told Blossom. "I plan to serve in about fifteen minutes."

"Cluck," Blossom said.

Mother turned to Uncle Wolfram. "If you want anything to eat you'd better bring her out of it," she told him.

Uncle Wolfram snapped his fingers thrice. "You are no longer a chicken," he said to Blossom.

"Squawk," Blossom said. "Cluck cluck cluck cluck cluck. Cluck."

"Darn it," Uncle Wolfram said.

"Try again," Mother told him. Uncle Wolfram snapped his fingers at Blossom.

"Cluck," Blossom said.

"That will do, Blossom," Mother said firmly. "No more nonsense, if you please." Mother snapped her fingers three times. "Blossom!" she said.

Blossom blinked and emerged from her trance. "What happened?" she asked. "Did I go under?"

"You were an excellent subject, Blossom," Mother said.

"Now I think you had best go upstairs and finish making your potato salad."

"Yes, Mrs. Trepel," Blossom said. She went back upstairs to the kitchen. Outside of an occasional cluck or squawk she spent the rest of the evening bustling about and humming to herself. At midnight the last of the guests said good-bye and left.

"It was a lovely party, Blossom," Mother said. "The refreshments were delicious, especially the potato salad."

"Thank you, Mrs. Trepel," Blossom said. "I always enjoy the magic parties. Cluck."

"Go to bed, Blossom," Mother said, sighing. "You can finish the dishes in the morning. And don't stay up half the night listening to the 'Milkman's Matinee' either," she added.

Blossom loved to dance. She had won honorable mention in the *Daily News* Harvest Moon Ball dancing with her boy friend, "Pal" Palderazzi.

"Jitterbug was our specialty," Blossom said. She sighed reminiscently. "One thing I had to hand it to Pal, he sure could dance."

Joyce and I adored listening to Blossom tell about her blighted romance with Pal.

"He was the best-looking guy you ever saw," Blossom said. "But like all Latins he was hot-blooded. He coulden keep his hands off the broads. He'd screw a snake if it had a skirt on."

"Tell how he tried to kill you in Roseland Ballroom," little Joyce begged.

"We were dancing in Roseland," Blossom said, "cheek to cheek, nice an' easy, when all of a sudden I don't know what come over me but I says to him, 'Pal, are you still seein' that horsy broad named Vivian from the steam table at Schrafft's?'"

"Then what happened, Blossom?" Joyce asked, as if we both didn't know. We had heard the story a dozen times. It never palled.

"Pal stops dancin' like somebody slugged him on the head," Blossom said. "He bares his teeth and gives me this crazy look. Let me tell you, I was scared."

"Show how he bared his teeth and looked crazy, Blossom," I said.

Blossom bared her teeth and looked crazy. Joyce and I shivered.

"Pal says to me," Blossom went on, "he says, 'I ever hear you mention Vivian from the steam table's name again I'll fix your wagon good, Blossom Hruska!' So I guess what happened next I asked for it, but I coulden help myself."

She paused. "Tell what happened next!" Joyce urged her. "Tell about when he pulled out the knife!"

"I says to him, 'You can't order me around, Pal Palderazzi, I ain't your slave. I'll mention Vivian from the steam table's name as much as I want. I'll say it till hell freezes over if I like. Vivian from the steam table! Vivian from the steam table!'"

Here Blossom dropped her voice to a near whisper.

"Pal pulls this knife out of his pants pocket," Blossom said dramatically. She pulled an imaginary knife out of an imaginary pants pocket. "He sticks this knife against my throat like this," she went on, sticking the imaginary knife against Joyce's throat, "and he says, 'Blossom, you ever mention that name again I'll kill you!'"

At this point Mother came into the kitchen and wanted to know what Blossom was doing. Joyce said, "She's telling how her boy friend tried to kill her in Roseland Ballroom, Mama."

"I've asked you not to tell the children that story, Blossom," Mother said. "It gives little Joyce terrible nightmares."

"I don't care, Mama, I like to have terrible nightmares," Joyce said earnestly. "Blossom, finish the story. Tell what happened after he stuck the knife in your throat."

"I run into the ladies' room screaming my head off," Blossom said. "The management called the cops and threw the bum out. I never seen him again."

"And good riddance to bad rubbish, Blossom," Mother said. "You're much better off without him."

"Yeah, I suppose," Blossom said, without much conviction. "I wrote a letter to the 'Voice of the People' column in the *News* asking if anybody knew the whereabouts of a certain Pal Palderazzi to get in touch. The *News* never even printed the letter."

Blossom and Delphine, the O'Gorsky's maid, were friends. They spent their days off together manicuring each other's nails in the morning and in the afternoon going off to Coney Island.

"We just bum around," Blossom told Mother. "Eat a coupla hot dogs, some cotton candy, get our pictures taken in one of them six-for-a-quarter booths. Delphine gets herself tattooed once in a while."

"Tattooed!" Mother cried. Blossom said only tiny little tattoos and not where it showed.

"She has a coupla hearts on the soles of her feet," Blossom explained. "Last week she got a real small anchor put down here." Blossom showed Mother where Delphine had got the real small anchor put. "It's kinda cute," Blossom said.

"I am very much surprised at Delphine and I certainly hope you don't plan to get yourself tattooed also," Mother said to Blossom.

"Delphine said it didn't hurt," Blossom said, "and the guy only charged her five bucks."

Blossom stayed with our family until we moved from Brooklyn to Great Neck, Long Island.

"Mr. Lupewitz don't want me to go to Great Neck," Blossom told Mother. Mr. Lupewitz was a widowed upholsterer. "He wants me to marry him and stay here in Brooklyn," Blossom said. "He's crazy about me."

She sighed. "I suppose I ought to marry him," she said.

Mother was concerned. "But do you love him, Blossom?" she asked.

"I dunno," Blossom said. "I guess so."

"Is he a marvelous dancer like Pal was?" Joyce wanted to know.

"He don't dance at all," Blossom said.

Mother told Joyce that Mr. Lupewitz was a fine man with a thriving upholstery business and whether or not he was a marvelous dancer had nothing to do with whether he would make Blossom a good husband.

"I hope you realize that too, Blossom," Mother said.

Blossom sighed again. "Yeah, I know," she said.

I never got a chance to meet Mr. Lupewitz but Joyce caught a glimpse of him just before we moved.

"What's he like?" I asked her curiously.

"He's kind of bald," Joyce said. "He's kind of fat, too."

"How does he act to Blossom?" I wanted to know.

"He acts real nice to her," Joyce said. "He acts like she could yell at him 'Vivian from the steam table!' till hell freezes over and he wouldn't stick a knife into her throat in a million years."

# 5

# *The Men in Her Life*

People half expected Mother to get married again after Daddy died. She had all the ingredients with which to make a good second marriage. She was lovely-looking (unless she happened to be wearing something perfectly good of mine that I had thrown away), she was a superb cook, and she knew a lot of men.

She knew boring Fred Mangold who was always dropping in at her house to eat up everything in sight and to tell stories about his three dead wives.

"Marry me, Mary," Fred begged Mother, but Mother refused.

"He's so boring," Mother told me. "Besides which, who wants to end up as possible former Mrs. Mangold number four?"

Fred gave up trying to talk Mother into marriage and asked her to go on a cruise to San Juan with him instead. She refused the cruise too. Fred went anyway and met a widow from Portland during a free Bossa Nova lesson aboard and married her instead.

When Mother heard the news she said, "Every pot has a cover."

Mr. Immanuel Corona had been a banker who all his life had secretly desired to be a house painter. Now that he had reached what he referred to as his Golden Years, he had decided to become one.

"I've hired Corona to paint the exterior of the house," Mother told me early in the spring. "I've decided to have it painted white this time."

Corona painted the house white all right, starting at the front and going all the way around and painting everything he came to along the way.

"He doesn't seem to be able to distinguish between doors or windows or stoops or trim," Mother told me, in near despair. "If it's attached to the house, Corona paints it."

Mother tried to tell Corona that she wanted only the house itself painted, but it didn't do much good. He said "Sure, I understand, Mrs. Trepel, house only! Right-O!" Then he painted the house and the azaleas bordering the house and a lawnmower that was leaning up against the house and he also painted poor darling Nellie, who happened to be asleep in the kitchen window box when Corona came around to it.

"Why do you put up with Corona?" I asked Mother. Mother was trying futilely to remove the white paint from Nellie's black fur with a mixture of turpentine and tomato juice. Corona had advised Mother that turpentine and tomato juice was, in his experience, a good combination for getting paint off of cats. Corona was wrong.

"I'll tell you why I put up with him," Mother answered me. "I put up with him because at least he shows up for work when he says he will, not like that rat Maynard."

Maynard was the gardener. His full name was Maynard P. Maynard but to Mother he was that rat Maynard, just as Nellie was poor darling Nellie.

"Today is Friday," Mother went on, dabbing at Nellie with the sponge. "That rat Maynard swore to me he'd be here last Monday. I haven't seen hide nor hair of him." Nellie growled in her throat. "Hold still, poor darling," Mother told her.

The lawn kept on growing whether that rat Maynard showed up or not. By the time he did show up the grass was too high for him to mow alone so he brought along two assistants. One assistant walked in front of the power mower picking up twigs and stones. The other assistant walked behind, raking up clippings. Nobody walked quickly.

"It's maddening," Mother would say, watching the classic *pas-de-trois* taking place on her lawn. The reason it was maddening was because that rat Maynard got paid by the hour. "They've been here since morning and they haven't even started the back yard yet," Mother said.

Besides house painters and gardeners and plumbers like Racovic, who spoke of himself always as "we" as though he were the British royal family or the editor of the New York *Times*—"We will do our best to fix the faucet drip, Mrs. Trepel, if we have the time"—Mother also knew a lot of men in show business.

Of these, Cyril Ritchard was her favorite. Cyril occupied a home across the river from Mother's house. Cyril and Mother were genuinely fond of each other in spite of the fact that they almost drove each other mad.

"Your mother is a wonderful woman, Irene, my dear," Cyril would tell me, "but one doesn't dare to pause for breath when one is in the same room with her. I hope you notice that she has just interrupted me in the middle of my anecdote about Sir Laurence Olivier."

"You take such dreadfully long pauses when you're talking, Cyril," Mother would say. "I certainly never intended to interrupt your anecdote. I thought surely you had finished."

"It is impossible not to take long pauses precisely because of your interruptions, Mary dear," Cyril said. "When I speak of your interruptions I include, of course, your asides, your nonsequiturs, and your frequent excursions back and forth into the kitchen."

> *The scene is Mother's living room. Several guests are present, including Cyril Ritchard. The conversation has touched lightly on literature and the arts and now turns to the theater.*

CYRIL: A rather amusing thing happened after my matinee yesterday. I had a—

MOTHER: Have you all seen Cyril's new show? It's marvelous.

CYRIL: Thank you, Mary dear. Yesterday after the matinee performance I had a surprise visitor backstage— Cornelia Otis Skinner—

MOTHER: That's funny, because only yesterday I was reading a book about her father, Otis Skinner.

CYRIL: Cornelia arrived backstage un—

MOTHER: Terribly boring book.

CYRIL: Cornelia arrived unannounced—as a matter of fact I had believed her to be abroad with—

MOTHER: I've always felt that Cornelia Otis Skinner is one of the most talented actresses on the stage today.

CYRIL: Yes. She is. As I was saying, Cornelia arrived backstage and my valet, Simpson, not recognizing—

MOTHER: That Simpson never recognizes anybody. I recall one Halloween when Chris—(*aside to other guests*) Chris is my oldest grandchild. She holds the highest Ph.D. degree ever granted to a woman in biochemistry. Or do I mean biology? At any rate Chris is a professor at the University of California in San Francisco, not the one at Berkeley; it's a hotbed of radicals that Berkeley campus, they ought to be ashamed of themselves, at any rate where was I? Oh yes, there's a photograph of Chris on the mantel in her white smock, yes we're all very proud of her indeed—Chris was five years old at the time I'm telling about and dressed up as a witch for Halloween and she rang your doorbell, Cyril, and Simpson answered the door and said, formally, "Mr. Ritchard is at dinner, miss. Whom shall I say is calling?"

(*General laughter from guests. Cyril waits, with an Early Christian martyr's smile, until the laughter dies away.*)

CYRIL: *As* I was saying, Mary dear, Simpson thought at first that Cornelia was one of those dear matinee ladies from New Jersey so he called to me—

MOTHER: Cyril, let me get you a cold drink.

CYRIL: No, thank you. Simpson called to me and said "Mr. Ritchard, a person is here to see you." I had of course recognized Cornelia's voice and decided to play a little joke—

MOTHER: How about a nice gin and tonic, Cyril? Your throat must be dry from all this talking. It won't take me a minute. Don't you dare go on with your story until I get back. I want to hear every word.

(*Mother exits into the kitchen.*)

CYRIL: (*Hastily taking advantage of her absence*) I said to Simpson, turning and scowling at him with mock ferocity, "Simpson, I forbid any persons—"

(*Mother returns from kitchen.*)

MOTHER: There doesn't seem to be any gin left in the liquor cupboard but I found half a bottle of lovely Manischewitz Kosher wine. (*Cyril cannot help shuddering slightly.*) Never mind, Cyril, plenty of British men drink Kosher wine. It's delicious. Sir Laurence Olivier who is such a great friend of yours happens to drink it all the time.

CYRIL: (*Momentarily sidetracked from his Cornelia Otis Skinner anecdote*) Larry Olivier drinks Kosher wine? I never knew that. How did you happen to discover this information, may I inquire, Mary dear?

MOTHER: Never mind, I discovered it. (*Probably under a dryer in the beauty parlor which is where she discovered Richard Burton's grandmother.*)

CYRIL: Well, as I was saying, I said to Simpson with mock ferocity, "Simpson, I forbid any persons to enter my dressing room!"

MOTHER: What an amusing story, Cyril! I can imagine the expression on Simpson's face when you said it. (*To other guests*) Unless you know Simpson you can't really appreciate Cyril's anecdote because Simpson is so—

CYRIL: (*Coldly*) I. Am. Not. Quite. Finished. With. My. Story. Mary. Dear.

MOTHER: Oh, Cyril, weren't you? You took such a long pause I was quite sure you had finished.

Of course Cyril did exactly the same sort of thing to Mother when they were in Cyril's living room at *his* house, Lone Rock.

At Lone Rock Cyril also had the advantage of the presence of Trim, his French poodle, who performed cute tricks like playing dead dog or fetching Cyril's slippers while Mother was talking, thus effectively ruining her punch lines.

The friendship between Cyril and Mother had begun

years before, while Daddy was still alive. It started with Mother's homemade tomato soup.

Cyril had moved into Lone Rock for the same reason that a lot of other show-business people had moved into summer and weekend homes in Ridgefield—for some peace and privacy. Ridgefield was the antidote for their hectic lives in New York City.

Cyril had made doubly sure of his peace and privacy, he thought, by purchasing a house on the banks of the Norwalk River. He had been in residence at his new retreat less than a day when he happened to glance out his front window to see Mother advancing up the path from the river, carrying a pot of something.

"Oh, damn," Cyril said. He didn't know that the woman with the pot was Mother; he knew only that some strange female was invading his peace and privacy and was probably going to demand an autograph into the bargain.

"How in the name of heaven did she get here?" Cyril wondered aloud. "Could she possibly have come swimming across the Norwalk River?"

What Cyril didn't know was that the river was hardly more than a stream at the point where his house and Mother's perched on opposite banks. A series of stepping stones spanned the water between the two banks. Nellie and The Prince frequently used these stones in their travels back and forth. "Well, I know the cats are dead for sure this time," Mother would say darkly. "They haven't been home for days. They have drowned in the Norwalk River." (See *Glossary*)

Mother rang Cyril's doorbell.

"Damn!" Cyril said again. He ducked down to the floor behind his front door. He crouched there, hardly breathing, waiting for whoever it was to go away.

Mother rang the doorbell. "Anyone home?" Mother

called. Mother, on her part, had no idea that an eminent actor had moved into Lone Rock and was crouched in hiding behind his door. Mother simply wanted to make a neighborly gesture to whoever had moved in. She had spotted the moving van leaving that morning, and that was all.

Mother rang and rang and at last she said, "Well, whoever bought the place must be down in the village shopping." She left the pot on the front doorstep and went back home across the river.

When he was sure the woman was gone, Cyril cautiously opened his door. He picked the pot up in order to toss it away into the woods when he happened to catch a whiff of the soup.

"Ah?" Cyril said. He took another sniff of the pot's contents. "Well, well, what have we here?" Cyril said. He carried the pot inside and set it down on his kitchen table. "I shall just fetch a spoon," Cyril said.

He finished every drop of the soup. Then he went outside to his front stoop in the hope that whoever the woman was who had brought it to him would come back bringing a great deal more.

She came back the next day. As soon as Cyril saw her approaching he sprang out and said, "Mrs. er—uh—my dear lady, I am so happy to see you. That pot of soup you so kindly left for me yesterday was—"

"Did you like it?" Mother said, interrupting Cyril for the first, but not the last, time. "Well, I'm glad, because it's an old recipe that I've made for years that Miss Parker who was a spinster and lived in East Haddam near my grandmother's house gave to me."

It was the beginning of a beautiful friendship.

In case you are interested in striking up a meaningful

relationship with an eminent actor, here is the recipe for
the soup:

### Miss Parker's Tomato Soup

Three quarts sliced tomatoes
Six onions, sliced fine
Two quarts water
Six tablespoons sugar
Three teaspoons salt
One-half teaspoon pepper
Thirty whole cloves
Few sprays parsley

As you can see from the size of the first ingredient—three
quarts of tomatoes—the soup can be made only in late
summer when tomatoes are plentiful and inexpensive. The
tomatoes should always be slightly overripe. No, you can't
use canned tomatoes. Canned tomatoes! My mother would
turn in her grave!

Boil the above ingredients until done. I don't know exactly when "done" is. When I asked Mother she said,
"Done is when it's done." After it is done, add six tablespoons butter and six tablespoons cornstarch. Boil again
until thick. I don't know how thick. Thick!

When serving, add to each bowl of soup one tablespoon
whipped cream. Fresh sweet whipped cream, not that stuff
out of a pressure can. Fresh! It's important to add the
cream because it brings out the delicate flavor of the soup.

Mother used to give me jars of her tomato soup to take
home with me, but she never trusted me about the fresh
whipped cream.

"Be sure and add a tablespoon of whipped cream after
you heat up the soup," Mother said.

"I will," I said. "You've already told me about the

whipped cream a thousand times, for God's sake, Mother!"

"Never mind," Mother said. "I know you."

What she meant was "The minute you get home you'll sit down and eat the soup right out of my jar because it's too much trouble to heat it up in a saucepan like a civilized person, to say nothing of taking the time to whip a little cream in a mixing bowl because it would mean, God forbid, having to wash up the saucepan and the bowl in the sink afterward, to say nothing of a soup plate and probably use a brand-new scouring pad on the saucepan into the bargain like a drunken sailor."

She was absolutely right, too.

That's the end of the recipe. The recipe makes a great deal of soup. I don't know how much exactly. Mother used to make it in her biggest kettle. Her biggest kettle was *big*.

If you make too much soup, at least it can be frozen.

# 6

# From Whence
# and Whither?

My daughter Chris is interested in genetics. Genetics is her
field of specialization at the College of Medicine of the
University of California in San Francisco, where she is a
professor.

Personally I feel that if God had meant us to fool around
with our genes He would have put them someplace where
we could get at them easily, like in our elbows, but what do
I know, I'm only a mother.

I have never actually understood what Chris does out
there at the University of California where they keep the
genes, but I assume she was thinking along genetic lines
when she asked me to reconstruct the family tree and send
it to her.

"Put down who came from where," she said. "Also
when, if possible, and how."

Chris's first American ancestor on her paternal, or WASP
side, came from England. His name was John Howland
and he arrived aboard the *Mayflower*. Howland was the

ship's cooper and was in charge of the *Mayflower*'s cargo of wine barrels.

Howland distinguished himself in the annals of Plymouth Colony by falling overboard while the *Mayflower* was still at anchor in the harbor.

Howland married a number of times and produced a great many children, who in turn produced a great many more children.

One day I was touring the Plymouth Colony Restoration in Massachusetts and I said to the guide in the Howland House, "My daughter is a descendant of the original John Howland who arrived on the *Mayflower*," and the guide said, "Who isn't?"

Chris's great-grandparents on her maternal, or *at least*, side, came from Russia. They had fled the pogroms and arrived with little more than the clothes on their backs. At least they arrived.

My father's side of the family made their way to Brooklyn and went into the retail flower business. The five boys peddled flowers from a pushcart on the East Side and turned over all their earnings to Grandpa Trepel, who had been an aristocrat back in Russia and didn't believe in soiling his hands with work of any sort.

Grandpa Trepel had a monumental temper. He ruled his household like a czar. He never heard of Women's Lib. If he had, he would have hurled a chicken at it. Grandpa was a great chicken hurler, and once when Grandma Trepel displeased him in some innocuous manner he hurled the main course of the dinner she had prepared for him—half a roast chicken—down the toilet.

Grandma Trepel put up with Grandpa for seventy-seven years. She had been married to him at fourteen, sight unseen, the marriage having been arranged by both sets of parents when the children were born, which was the custom in the old country.

Grandma eventually appeared on our doorstep one day and said to Mother, "I'm through. I've left him. Let him cook his own chickens from now on. I'm never going back to him again—never!"

"But, Mama," my mother said to her, "you've been married for such a long time—seventy-seven years. You are ninety-one years old, Mama. Papa is ninety-two years old. Why have you decided to leave him now?"

"Because," Grandma Trepel announced firmly, "enough is enough."

Mother's side of the family also fled from Russia. This branch settled on the banks of the Connecticut River in the picturesque farming town of East Haddam. The Goldsteins were the first Jewish family in East Haddam and the natives hardly knew what to make of them, especially of Great-grandma Goldstein, the matriarch of the clan.

Grandma Goldstein spoke only Yiddish and never mastered more than two English phrases to the end of her life, although she was a resident of East Haddam for seventy-five years, nearly as many years as Grandma Trepel had put up with Grandpa Trepel.

The two phrases were "Gerrodahere" and "A klug on Columbus."

"Gerrodahere!" Grandma Goldstein would shout, brandishing her stick at stray cats, small children, and occasionally at Grandpa Goldstein himself. "A klug on Columbus!" ("A black day on Columbus!") was reserved for a wider range of Grandma Goldstein's enemies and included not only stray cats, children, and Grandpa Goldstein, but also all bill collectors, reform rabbis, and the governor of Connecticut.

Like Darby and Joan, Grandma Goldstein and Grandpa Trepel were made for each other. It is the fault of the planets in their courses that the two never even met.

Genetically, though, they are welded together for eternity. Both have re-emerged miraculously unto the second and third generations in their mutual descendant Christine, who answers long-distance telephone calls from me, her mother, in the manner of a deep-sea monster being stirred untimely in its lair.

"You sound sort of cross, darling," Mother says over the wire.

"Naturally I sound cross!" Christine says. She grits her teeth. It is all she can do to keep herself from shouting "Gerrodahere!" at Mother. "It happens to be not even six o'clock in the morning here in San Francisco!" she says.

If she had a chicken handy she would hurl it down a toilet.

Mother says apologetically, "I'm sorry, darling, I always forget the three-hour time difference between Ridgefield and San Francisco."

What Mother really longs to say is, "Fine thanks I get for the sleepless nights I spent lugging warm milk and stuffed bears to your crib. A klug on Columbus!", but Mother is not so dumb. Mother may not have learned many lessons out there in the great big classroom of life, but one thing she has learned is to keep her mouth shut.

And to smile a lot.

Chris and Don were married to each other in a cloud of white tulle and five bridesmaids, after which they left for graduate school at the University of Wisconsin where they were going to live happily ever after.

I decided to pay them a surprise visit. (First lesson in the classroom of life: Do not pay surprise visits to your children. Mothers! Attention! No surprise visits!)

"Surprise, Don!" I said. I had flown out to Madison, registered at the Badger Arms Hotel, and dialed their number. "This is Mother, Don," I said.

The masculine voice that had answered the phone said, "I am not Don. I am Egon."

Egon? Who was Egon?

"I would like to speak to my daughter, Chris," I told Egon.

"Just a minute," Egon said. I heard him put the phone down and then I heard him call "Somebody's mother wants to speak to Chris!"

Somebody's mother?

"Mother?" Chris's voice came on the wire. In the background I could hear music, faintly Arabic in tone. "Where are you, Mother?" Chris said.

"Surprise!" I said again. "I'm here in Madison at the Badger Arms."

"Oh, God," Chris said. "Well, stay there, I'll be right over."

"How is Don?" I said. Chris said, "How is who?" "Don," I said. "Your husband."

"Don is fine," Chris said. "Listen, Mother, why didn't you let me know you were coming out here to Madison?"

"I wanted to surprise you," I said.

"You certainly did," Chris said.

I went down to the Badger Arms lobby and waited for Chris. She appeared dressed in what I took to be a Turkish beggar's castoff coat and one of Greta Garbo's old hats. She was also wearing army shoes.

"Hello, darling," I said. We embraced. "Let's go into the coffee shop and have coffee," I said.

We went into the Badger Arms coffee shop and sat down at a table.

"Black coffee, please," Chris told the waitress. "How

is Grandma?" she asked me. "The weather here has been vile. Don and I are separated. Please pass the sugar."

I passed the sugar. "Don't look so stricken, Mother," Chris said. "It's all very amicable and Don and I are still good friends. I got the Chevrolet. He got the Yamaha."

"The who?" I asked. Chris told me that a Yamaha was a Japanese motorcycle.

"Don got that," she told me again.

"Very nice," I said. "Wonderful. And who, may I inquire, got the monogrammed silver and the monogrammed punchbowl from Tiffany's and the monogrammed towels, to say nothing of your uncle Wolfram Trepel's electric frying pan, all of which are stored upstairs in my attic this very minute back in Connecticut waiting until you and Don set up housekeeping?"

I paused for breath. Chris set down her cup and said, "I knew you were going to make a scene! I knew it!" I objected. I said I wasn't making a scene.

"Well, you have this terrible frowning expression on your face," Chris said. "I can't stand it. I want you to look happy!"

I fixed what I hoped was a reasonable approximation on my face of a mother's happy smile on hearing the news that her only child's marriage has broken up.

"There," I said. "I'm smiling. Now, be so good as to tell me what happened between you and Don."

Chris said it just hadn't worked out between them, marriage, she meant, and they had separated and she, Chris, had moved into a marvelous tumbledown old house where she was now living with a bunch of really great people.

"Is it a commune?" I asked.

"Oh, *Mother!*" Chris said. "It's not a commune! Good grief! It's just this bunch of people—me and Egon and

Abdul and Abdul's girl friend from Nigeria—there you go, frowning again."

"No, no, not frowning," I assured her. "Happy. Smiling." I managed to summon up a sickly grin. "See? Smiling!" I said.

Chris said would I like to see this marvelous tumble-down house and meet all these really great people? I said yes, of course, so we got into a taxicab.

"Here we are," Chris said. The ride had taken about ten minutes. We got out of the cab. I paid the driver. "Isn't it a marvelous old house?" Chris said to me.

Several automobiles in various stages of decay were parked in the marvelous old house's marvelous old drive-way. A goat was tethered on the front grass.

"The goat belongs to Egon," Chris said. "Egon is into the cottage industry bit this year. He makes fabulous cheese out of goat's milk."

I said, "Goat cheese! Yum! Sounds marvelous!"

Chris said, "Mother, before we go inside the house I want to make one final appeal to you to please try and take a positive viewpoint of the situation. Try to be happy about it."

"I will try," I said.

"And one more thing," Chris said. "I hope you don't mind, but it would be better if you didn't mention to Egon and Abdul that you wrote the book the Lucille Ball televi-sion series is based on. Egon and Abdul despise television."

I smiled happily.

We went into the house. "This is the living room," Chris said. "We got the furniture from the Society of St. Vincent de Paul. Don't you love the sofa?"

"I love it," I said. "It's really marvelous."

"Don't sit down on it!" Chris warned, too late. A cloud of

old Society of St. Vincent de Paul dust rose from the sofa's innards. I got up hastily.

"And this is the kitchen," Chris said, leading me into the kitchen. "I'm sorry it's such a mess with the cat sleeping in the sink and everything."

"No, no, I like a kitchen that's homey-looking," I said.

"We haven't washed the dishes for a week because we hate to disturb Cleopatra," Chris said. "She's expecting kittens and the sink is the only place she seems to want to sleep."

I said, "Kittens! How sweet!"

"After they're born we could ship you one," Chris said. "Egon could build a crate for it and ship it by air express."

"Well, I'll let you know about shipping a kitten, okay?" I said. I took a good look at Cleopatra. "Under no circumstances allow Egon to ship me a kitten unless you hear from me definitely, understand?" I said.

We went upstairs. "This is my bedroom," Chris said. "Do you like it?"

"I like it," I said. "I really do. Where's the bed?"

"Mother!" Chris said.

"I'm not criticizing," I said hastily. "I was merely wondering. Actually now that I see a bedroom without a bed I think it's quite attractive. Without a bed, I mean."

Chris said the bed was that mattress on the floor. The mattress had a batik throw over it.

"Medical statistics have proven that it's much healthier for people to sleep on the floor," Chris said. "Thoreau slept on the floor at Walden."

"So he did," I said, smiling happily at the thought of Thoreau sleeping on the floor at Walden. I was beginning to fear permanent deformation of the face from so much happy smiling.

We went downstairs to the kitchen again.

"Would you like something to eat, Mother?" Chris asked me. She opened the refrigerator. "There's nothing much here but a sort of stalish bagel and some goat's milk cheese," she said. "I could make you a sandwich of them."

I said a sandwich of stalish bagel and goat's milk cheese would be fine and my only daughter made me such a sandwich and not only that, I ate it, and not only that but I said about it, "Yum!"

Chris and I sat down in the marvelous Society of St. Vincent de Paul living room. I noticed an old wicker baby carriage in a corner. I smiled at it happily.

"Let's talk about things," Chris said to me. "I mean, let's talk about interesting things like what's new at home and let's kindly try to stay away from subjects that will lead to a scene, okay?"

"Okay," I said. I tried to think about something interesting at home for a mother to talk about and yet not lead to a scene such as talk about how upstairs in my attic at home this very minute, in addition to the monogrammed silver and the monogrammed towels and the monogrammed punchbowl and Uncle Wolfram Trepel's electric frying pan, was also Chris's wedding gown preserved for future generations in a corrugated cardboard packing case.

"Let's see," I said. "Well, your uncle Wolfram is taking guitar lessons." It wasn't a terribly interesting thing but it seemed safe. I was wrong.

"Uncle *Wolfram?*" Chris said. "At his age? How ridiculous!"

"What does age have to do with it?" I inquired. "Robert Frost was playing the guitar the day before he died at the age of eighty-nine."

"Your side of the family is so peculiar, Mother," Chris said.

"How do you mean, 'peculiar'?" I said, bristling. Chris

said like Grandma Trepel for instance leaving Grandpa Trepel at the age of ninety-one.

"And now Uncle Wolfram taking guitar lessons at seventy-seven," Chris said. "Honestly!"

"Haydn wrote his finest works when he was past sixty," I told her.

"Yes, and Mozart wrote his first opera at twelve," Chris said. "If you don't mind, Mother, would you please not mention to Egon and Abdul when they get here about Uncle Wolfram and his guitar."

So when Egon and Abdul got there I not only refrained from mentioning about Uncle Wolfram and his guitar, but I also refrained from mentioning how Grandma Trepel had left her husband at the age of ninety-one, and not only that but I also refrained from telling them that I had written the book on which the Lucille Ball television series was based.

A klug on Columbus.

# 7

# Arise Already, Workers

"Bandiera rosa tirirumvira
Euviva Communismo et libertal"

Know what that is? It's the Italian Communist Party Anthem and lucky for me that the Senate Internal Security Committee wasn't strolling past my bathroom window this morning because I was singing it at the top of my lungs.

How would I have explained to the committee?

"Are you seriously asking us to believe, Mrs. Kampen, that you learned the Italian Communist Party Anthem—both the Italian *and* the English versions—at a summer camp in the Pocono Mountains of Pennsylvania?"

"Yes, sir, it's true. Camp Pa-Ma-Mau."

"You are quite sure you did not learn the anthem in some underground Communist cell?"

"No, sir. It was at Camp Pa-Ma-Mau."

"Is Pa-Ma-Mau by any chance a code name for the U.S.S.R.?"

"No, sir. Honestly, sir, I was an Intermediate Squaw in

Beaver Tent when I learned it. I was fourteen at the time."

"A likely story."

"I can hardly blame you gentlemen for not believing me. I can hardly believe it myself. My parents—lifelong registered Republicans—all unknowingly shipped me off to a Communist camp for the summer. Not only that, they also forked over a fee of two hundred dollars for the privilege."

If Mother and Daddy had had the slightest inkling that Pa-Ma-Mau was run by Communists they would have been horrified. They both detested communism and anything even remotely connected with it.

"Those Communists ought to be ashamed of themselves," Mother said. "Carrying on the way they do! It's disgusting."

"What do they do that's disgusting, Mama?" my little sister, Joyce, wanted to know.

"Running around the lawn in their nightgowns," Mother said. "They ought to be arrested."

Mother got her ideas about the way Communists behaved by observing Aunt Tillie Trepel, the family radical. Aunt Tillie wore thong sandals and had been known to dance on the lawn in her nightgown when the mood seized her.

Poor Mother! She didn't even suspect that she was sending her oldest daughter straight into the arms of the Communist Party for one entire summer.

The advertisement for Pa-Ma-Mau that caught Mother's eye in the New York *Times* said nary a word about communism. It said: "Swimming. Canoeing. Dedicated Staff. Spotless Kitchens. Nestled high in the pure air of the Pocono Mountains."

"It sounds exactly what we've been looking for for Irene this summer," Mother told Daddy. I had never been sent to summer camp before. "Just look at the lovely photograph of Lake Pa-Ma-Mau," Mother said. She handed him the advertisement.

" 'Beautiful Lake Pa-Ma-Mau'," Daddy read. " 'Legend tells us this crystal-clear lake sparkling like a jewel on the shores of Camp Pa-Ma-Mau was named after the fabled Indian Princess Pa-Ma-Mau who leaped to her death from unrequited love.' "

Much later I discovered that beautiful Lake Pa-Ma-Mau was actually named after Pa and Ma Yerevan, the owners of the camp, and their son Maurice, the head counselor. By the time I found out the truth it was too late. I was already an Intermediate Squaw in Beaver Tent, chanting the Italian Communist Party Anthem and vying for the weekly Pa-Ma-Mau Good Sportsmanship medal.

Daddy put down the advertisement for Pa-Ma-Mau with satisfaction and said, "I'll send them a check for the deposit at once."

Like Mother, Daddy too thought the Communists were all safely over in Moscow dancing on the lawn in their nightgowns. He would have been appalled to know that they were not only nestled cozily in the Pocono Mountains, but that he was about to send them a lot of money.

"I don't want to go away to summer camp," I said sulkily. I detested outdoor sports, especially swimming and canoeing. "I want to stay home this summer with you and Daddy and dear little Joyce," I said, but Mother saw right through me.

"She wants to stay home this summer to hang around the house with her nose in a book," she told Daddy, "listening to Blossom tell how her boy friend tried to stab her with a knife in Roseland Ballroom."

"I do not," I said.

"It will do you a world of good to get two months of fresh air and healthy exercise," Mother said.

"I'm afraid to go to camp," I said. Mother asked me what I was afraid of. I thought for a moment. "I'll drown in Lake Pa-Ma-Mau," I said.

"You won't drown," Mother said. "They won't allow it."

"I'll be homesick," I said. "Summer camp is expensive. I don't want to cost you and Daddy a lot of money." I tried desperately to think of additional reasons for my parents to keep me home. It never occurred to me, of course, to add "I will fall into the hands of the Communist Party."

"You're going to camp this summer and I don't want to hear another word about it," Mother said. "I think you might act a bit more grateful to Daddy and me for sending you away for a glorious vacation."

"I don't want to go away for a glorious vacation," I said. "All my friends are staying home. Cookie O'Gorsky is going to spend the summer learning how to be a manicurist by mail from Chicago. Why can't I stay home too?"

"You are going to Camp Pa-Ma-Mau," Mother said with finality, "and that is that."

Back in those days when a parent said, "That is that," that was that. I subsided.

The first hint of what goodies were in store for the summer came when I was delivered to Grand Central Station to board the Pa-Ma-Mau special train for Pennsylvania. That's when I got my first look at Pa and Ma Yerevan and their son Maurice.

Whatever summer camp owners are supposed to look like, I told myself, I'm pretty sure they're not supposed to look like the Yerevans.

Ma Yerevan wore culottes and a middy blouse in the camp colors—red and gold, naturally—and had her hair tied back with an old shoestring. Pa Yerevan was in golf knickers and Cossack blouse. Son Maurice was in unappetizing soiled tennis whites and had some sort of a scalp condition. He also drooled slightly when he talked.

All three Yerevans wore thong sandals.

"We're going to take advantage of time on the journey to Pennsylvania to learn some camp songs, campers," Maurice told us. "We'll start with a rousing marching tune which may be unfamiliar to some of you. All together now—repeat the words after me—

"'Arise you workers, fling to the breezes
The scarlet banner, the scarlet banner!
The scarlet banner triumphantly!'"

"One of our campers is not singing, Maurice," Ma Yerevan said. She pointed at me. "What is your name, camper?" she asked.

"Irene Trepel," I told her.

"At Pa-Ma-Mau everybody sings, Trepel," Ma Yerevan informed me. "It's what we call the Pa-Ma-Mau team spirit—all singing together. All!"

"Now I'm going to teach you the Italian version of the marching tune we've just learned, campers," Maurice told us. "Repeat after me—all together now."

"*All!*" Ma Yerevan said, gazing fiercely at me. "All means all!"

"The Italian version," Maurice began, "is entitled 'Bandiera Rosa' which means *scarlet banner*, and the first words are 'Bandiera rosa tirirumvira.' The correct pronunciation is 'Bahn-dee-year-ah. . . .'"

By the time the train arrived at Chacahoxie, Pennsylvania, our destination, Maurice had succeeded in teaching all us campers—*all!*—both the Italian and English versions of the anthem. We marched off the train in lock step, two hundred strong, and paraded through the streets of Chacahoxie to the waiting buses chanting, at the top of our lungs—

> "Bandiera rosa tirirumvira!
> Enviva Communismo et liberta!"

God knows what the residents of Chacahoxie made of it. I'm surprised they didn't send for the Pennsylvania National Guard.

"Your blouse is open!" Maurice chortled, pointing at me with a pudgy finger. I clutched at my middy. "Fooled you, fooled you, heh heh heh!" Maurice said, wetly.

Maurice spent a lot of time that summer destroying the future sex life of us nubile Beaver Tent squaws. We were at an impressionable age and we took Maurice seriously. Looking back on it, of course, he should have been identifiable immediately to any female past the age of twelve as a bona-fide sex pervert.

"I loathe and detest Maurice Yerevan," I confided to Squaw Elaine Gurwitz, my tent mate. "When I think of Maurice and then I think of Howie—" I shuddered. "It doesn't seem possible that they both belong to the same *sex*," I said.

Howie was waterfront counselor.

"Howie has the bluest eyes," I told Elaine. "Have you ever noticed his eyes? They're like—they're like—" I sighed. "They're so *blue*," I finished lamely.

I was in love for the first time in my life.

"Howie is a sophmore at C.C.N.Y.," Elaine said. "He's in pre-Law. He had a girl friend but they got into a big fight before he left to come up here to Pa-Ma-Mau."

"How do you know all that stuff?" I asked jealously.

"He told me," Elaine said.

I turned and walked out of the tent. Howie had never

spoken so much as a single word to me. He didn't know I
was alive and here he had been confiding his innermost
secrets to that nasty little Elaine Gurwitz.

"I hate her," I said to myself.

I turned and walked moodily in the direction of Lake Pa-
Ma-Mau where Princess Pa-Ma-Mau had leaped to her
death from unrequited love.

"I bet if I leaped to my death in that crumby old lake my
parents would be sorry they made me come to this crumby
old camp!" I said aloud.

"What was that, Squaw Trepel?" Ma Yerevan demanded, coming at me suddenly from around a tree.
"Talking to yourself, Squaw?"

I muttered something.

"I noticed that you were not present in the Social Hall
last night," Ma Yerevan went on. "Maurice was at his
most interesting."

Maurice was in the habit of giving lectures with titles
like "The Theory of Lenin's Ideology in Relation to Man-
ufacturing on the Kerch Peninsula" to the assembled
campers and illustrating his words with boring slides of
Ukrainian wheat harvesters.

"I didn't feel well," I told Ma Yerevan sullenly. This was
untrue. I had felt perfectly well. I had sneaked back to
Beaver Tent to write a long love poem to Howie.

"You missed Maurice's announcement concerning Play
Week," Ma Yerevan told me. At Pa-Ma-Mau, Play Week
didn't mean games. It meant drama.

"The highlight of this summer's Play Week will be an
original pageant depicting the working class struggle for
peace," Ma Yerevan said. She added, sternly, "With special
emphasis on the role of Camp Pa-Ma-Mau in said
struggle."

"Oh," I said. "Well, that's certainly interesting."

"Maurice emphasized that the pageant is a project in which all Pa-Ma-Mau campers—*all!*—are expected to co-operate," Ma informed me. "I trust you will keep that in mind." She gave a regal wave of her hand. "Go on your way, camper."

I went on toward the lake. When I got there, Howie was standing on the dock supervising a canoe test. When he caught sight of me, he beckoned.

I looked behind me, but he beckoned again.

Howie wanted me. Me!

"You're Irene Trepel, aren't you?" Howie said to me. I nodded dumbly. "Somebody told me you like to write poetry," he said.

I noticed that he had a tiny white scar at the corner of his mouth. It moved up and down when he spoke. I stared at it, entranced.

"The Yerevans have made me director of their goddam Play Week pageant," Howie told me. "I'm hereby appointing you to compose the lyrics for the dumb thing, okay?"

"Huh?" I said. Now that I was standing so close to him I saw that his eyes were even bluer than I had thought.

"The words," Howie said to me. "The words to the music for the pageant. I'm asking you to write them."

"Words?" I said. "What words?"

"The pageant," Howie explained patiently, "celebrating the goddam working-class struggle for peace with special emphasis on the role of this goddam camp."

"Oh, *that* pageant," I said. "Sure."

"You don't have to write any of the music," Howie told me. "Maurice is supplying the music. You only have to write the words."

"I will," I assured him fervently. "I'll write words, Howie." He smiled at me. His teeth were startlingly white against the tan of his face. "I will, Howie!" I said. "Write words, I mean."

"You'll have to write them fast," Howie said. "The pageant is scheduled for this Saturday night."

I wrote a lot of words. The music that Maurice supplied for the pageant consisted of a veritable *potpourri* of popular songs—popular in the Soviet Union, that is.

Maurice's songs had titles like "Red Army Forever," "Caucasus Mountains Nights," and "Azerbaijan, My Native Homeland, I Salute Thee."

To the tune of "Red Army Forever" I wrote the words:

> Pa-Ma-Mau forever
> Pa-Ma-Mau will never fail.
> Hail!

and to the tune of "Caucasus Mountains Nights" I wrote the words:

> Pocono mountain nights
> Bring beneficial delights
> Of marches far for glorious Pa-Ma-Mau
> We'll win. Yay!

and so on.

The pageant was produced under Howie's direction on Saturday night. Sunday morning, at reveille, it was discovered that Howie had vanished from the camp grounds.

"The poor lad had to be rushed back to New York with an inflamed appendix," Pa Yerevan explained. The truth, passed in whispers from tent to tent, was that Howie had been fired.

"Pa fired him," Elaine Gurwitz told me. "Pa is always firing Pa-Ma-Mau employees. He fired the cook and he fired a couple of the handymen and last summer he fired the camp rabbi."

I never saw Howie again. I was returned by the Yerevans to my parents in Brooklyn at the end of the summer with a heart still aching from unrequited love, like Princess Pa-Ma-Mau, and a head bursting from Communist propaganda.

"Welcome home, darling," Mother said, embracing me. She and Daddy had met me at Grand Central Station. Daddy kissed me. "We missed you terribly," he said.

"How come you look so pale?" Mother demanded, fixing me with a critical eye. I said it was because I had spent practically the entire summer shut up inside musty old Beaver Tent writing Communist songs.

"The only time they let us outside was when they marched us to the Social Hall to listen to lectures on how wonderful communism is from that hideous creep Maurice Yerevan," I said.

"I never heard anything so ridiculous," Mother said. "Why, only last week we received a lovely letter from the Yerevans telling us how splendidly you were doing in waterfront activities."

"They write the same letter to all the parents," I said. "They only do it so you'll send us back to horrible old Camp Pa-Ma-Mau again next summer and they can get more money to give to the Communists."

"That will do," Mother said. "It's bad enough that you didn't enjoy your lovely summer at Pa-Ma-Mau without your accusing the Yerevans of being Communists into the bargain."

"They are too Communists!" I said heatedly. "If you don't believe me I'll sing you one of the songs they taught us. It's the Italian Communist Party Anthem. Listen—'Arise you workers! Fling to the breezes! The scarlet banners! The scarlet banners! Arise—'"

"That will do!" Mother said. Several passers-by in the station had stopped to listen to my song. "I've never been so embarrassed," Mother said.

"I'm just trying to prove to you that you and Daddy sent me to a Communist camp—" I began, but Mother said, "That will do. I don't want to hear another word about Communists and that is that!"

I told you nobody would believe me.

I recovered from my unrequited love for Howie after a while and eventually I recovered from the Communists too, although that took longer, because the following autumn I was sent as a freshman to Abraham Lincoln High School in Brooklyn.

I am sorry to have to report that in those days Abraham Lincoln High School was another hotbed of communism. A good part of the curriculum was devoted to teaching us students how rotten everything in America was, how wonderful everything in the Soviet Union was going to be, how Thomas Jefferson kept slaves, and how George Washington had wooden teeth.

As if that wasn't enough, after I graduated from Lincoln, Mother and Daddy spent thousands of dollars to send me away to the University of Wisconsin, which in that period was under the direct control of the International Communist Party, according to Colonel Robert McCormick, publisher of the Chicago *Tribune*.

BARE RED LOVE NEST ON UW CAMPUS, the Colonel's headlines read. COMMIES FLUNKED ME, UW CO-ED CHARGES. BOLSHY TIES TO UW REGENTS REVEALED.

"What I can't understand," my daughter says to me, "is how you emerged from all this Communist indoctrination with political principles only slightly to the right of Louis the Fourteenth."

I can scarcely understand it myself. Indeed, the only remaining souvenir I carry from those formative years are the words to the Italian Communist Party Anthem.

Why can I not forget the song that Maurice Yerevan taught me on the train to Chacahoxie, Pennsylvania, so long ago? Why is it imbedded in my memory along with other useless trivia like my ex-husband's old army serial number (0826997) and the name of King Ethelred's successor to the British throne (Edmond Ironside)?

A klug on you, Maurice Yerevan, wherever you are.

# 8

## Abracadabra

I'm not sure how Women's Lib is going to feel about this, but I am currently the owner of a 100 per cent guaranteed love spell.

I am a magician's daughter—Daddy was president of the Parent Assembly of the Society of American Magicians for three consecutive terms—and magicians' daughters don't usually believe in love spells. We are brought up to be skeptical of all occult phenomena.

"Spirit rapping, automatic writing, and messages from the beyond can be reproduced by any competent professional magician with the use of run-of-the-mill sleight of hand skill and showmanship," Daddy said. "This also goes for table tilting, floating teacups, levitated trumpets, and Ouija board phenomenon."

Daddy's specialty in the magic world was mind reading, also known as second sight. Mother acted as his assistant.

"Tell the audience, if you please," Daddy would instruct Mother, who was blindfolded and in spangles, "exactly what picture the gentleman in the third row has drawn on his slate while you have been sitting onstage with your back to the audience unable to see and with absolutely no

means of communication with either myself or with anyone else in this theater."

"The gentleman has drawn a—is it a tent?" Mother
would say. "No, not a tent, but very much like a tent—just
one moment—the mists are fading—all becomes clearer—
the spirits are speaking to me from beyond the mists—"

"Exactly what is it the spirits are telling you, can you
describe it to the audience?" Daddy would say.

"I see—I see—the gentleman has drawn—yes! I see now!
A house!" Mother would say, hamming it up unmercifully.
"A house with three windows, a door, a chimney, smoke
coming from the chimney—it is beginning to fade—no, I
have caught one final glimpse—ah! Sitting before the door
of the house the gentleman has drawn a dog—a large
sheep dog!"

Wild applause from the audience. Mother would remove her blindfold and, bowing, she would toss it to the
spectators. Daddy, resplendent in white tie and tails,
would lead her to the center of the stage. Together they
would take bow after bow.

For a retail florist and a Jewish mother, it was heady
stuff.

"Harry Houdini himself started my interest in magic,"
Daddy told me. "The Houdinis lived across the street from
us in Brooklyn. I was only a little boy but he showed me the
rudiments of sleight of hand and taught me the principles
of misdirection. Misdirection is the basis of all magic."

Misdirection is the art of beguiling the audience into
looking at one thing when they want to look at another.

"Houdini was a master of misdirection," Daddy went on.
"He was a great showman. I longed to be a professional
magician too when I grew up."

It was not to be. Daddy, like his brothers before him,
found himself in the flower business. He never gave up his

avocation, though, and was considered by his peers to be a better magician than many of the practicing professionals.

"I invented the telephone trick for your mother so that she and I would have one mind-reading routine that no one else on earth could figure out," Daddy said. In the course of the telephone trick Mother, blindfolded, would locate for members of the audience preselected telephone numbers in any telephone directory in the United States.

In addition to locating secret telephone numbers, Mother could also hold audiences spellbound by revealing the exact amount of change in somebody's pocket, the serial number on a hidden dollar bill, and where the lady in the seventh row had hidden her pearl earrings for safe-keeping.

"The earrings are in—in—in—" Mother would say, "—just before you left your house this evening you went into your kitchen—no, your bedroom—no, kitchen it was—and put the earrings inside—inside—the breadbox standing in the kitchen window next to a potted geranium plant!"

Thunderous applause.

"I invented that one for your mother too," Daddy told me. "It's a good trick, if I say so myself, and your mother performs it magnificently. She's even convinced a few magicians that she really is able to read minds. Thank God, she can't!"

"Amen!" I answered.

Daddy also invented a number of illusions. The most famous of these was his rising-card trick. There are several rising-card tricks on the market, but Daddy's was the spookiest. A previously selected card taken from a sealed deck would rise from a goblet suspended in mid-air and, at Daddy's command, float over the heads of the audience. When Daddy gave the signal, the card gently drifted downward to the lap of the person who had selected it.

"Tell us how your father and mother do those tricks!" Joyce and I were asked by our friends, but we never would tell. Daddy had taught us that the magician's code of ethics is the magician's bible. To reveal the secret of any trick was underhanded and deplorable.

"And it might also deprive some magician of his livelihood," Daddy said.

"Besides," we told our friends, "once you knew the secret you wouldn't enjoy the trick any more. Most tricks are childishly simple once you are in on the explanation."

"It's fun to be fooled" was a slogan of the Society of American Magicians.

The Society, however, disapproved of fooling the public if it was done by fake mediums, spiritualists, and other charlatans. Houdini led the fight against phony occult phenomena all his life.

"Houdini wanted to believe in genuine spiritual manifestation," Daddy said. "He conscientiously investigated every claim brought to his attention, always hoping that this time the medium was honest and the phenomena unexplainable by natural means. He never found a medium who wasn't fraudulent. He never observed anything happen during a séance that he couldn't reproduce himself under similar conditions."

Daddy told of the time that a certain medium had contacted Houdini saying she had a message from Houdini's dead mother.

"She sounds genuine, Jack," Houdini said to Daddy. "She gave me reason to believe that she has an authentic message from my mother."

Houdini hurried to the medium's chambers. When

Daddy saw him the following day, Daddy said, "Was there a message from your mother, Harry?"

"Yes, there was a message," Houdini said, somewhat ruefully. "It was a long message full of loving endearments. The only trouble was that the message came through from the spirit world in English—faultless, grammatically perfect English. My mother never spoke any language except Yiddish till the day she died."

As president of the Society of American Magicians, Daddy was constantly being contacted by dabblers in the occult who reported that they had in their possession messages addressed to him from various departed persons. Among these persons were, at one time or another, Buffalo Bill, President Taft, Houdini himself, and, on one occasion, Grandma Goldstein.

Daddy conscientiously investigated every claim. Invariably it turned out that Buffalo Bill and President Taft had nothing much to communicate outside of a few desultory raps on a table. Houdini got through to Daddy with the information that if somebody's cousin Shirley wanted to find her lost cashmere sweater it could be located hanging from a hook in the back pantry.

"Grandma Goldstein kicked over a couple of chairs in the medium's parlor," Daddy said, "and also threw a teacup across the room but otherwise had nothing to say either in English or in Yiddish."

One day Daddy received a letter from somebody signing herself "Queen Hildegarde." Queen Hildegarde lived in Flatbush.

"She tells me she can read minds and foretell the future," Daddy said. "She wants me to visit her and have my future foretold. I suppose I must go."

Daddy made an appointment with Queen Hildegarde for the following Saturday. He showed up at her door with a semiopen mind. Queen Hildegarde ushered him into her parlor.

"Before I begin the séance to foretell your future," she said to Daddy, "allow me to fix you a cup of tea. Do you prefer cream or sugar?"

Daddy left quietly.

Daddy and Mother traveled with a U.S.O. Camp Shows unit entertaining Allied troops around the world during World War II.

The high spot of Daddy's magic act for the U.S.O. was the well-known rabbit-from-a-hat illusion in which the magician causes a rabbit to disappear and then produces it again from a seemingly empty top hat.

I don't think I am violating the code of ethics by pointing out that the trick necessitates the use of two rabbits—one to disappear, the other to reappear.

Mother and Daddy were in Bermuda, waiting in the wings to go on, during a camp show performance for Allied troops, nurses, and Red Cross girls.

"Jack!" Mother cried suddenly. "The rabbit!"

It was too late. One of Daddy's fluffy white rabbits had managed to open the latch and escape from its hutch. It vanished into the Bermuda night.

Daddy turned to the young G.I. who had been assigned as the unit's aide-de-camp and said to him, "Quickly, son—get me another rabbit."

"Another what, sir?" the G.I. said. Daddy said another rabbit. The G.I. gaped at him. The G.I. had aide-de-camped a lot of weird U.S.O. performers thus far and was skilled enough in getting them another spotlight or another set of guitar strings or another microphone, but another rabbit? And quickly?

"I need a rabbit to match this rabbit," Daddy said, taking the other fluffy white bunny from its hutch. "Hurry, son!"

"Yes sir!" the G.I. said. "One rabbit! At once, sir!" He raced off. Less than five minutes later he was back with a rabbit clutched in his arms.

"Here you are, sir!" the G.I. said to Daddy. "One rabbit, just as you ordered, sir!" He handed the rabbit to Daddy. The rabbit was brown, it weighed at least twenty pounds, and one of its ears was missing.

"And now—the Great Marvello assisted by the charming Miss Mary!" the master of ceremonies was announcing from the stage. Too late to do anything about the rabbits. Too late to do anything but bound on stage, bow, and begin the act.

"Watch closely, ladies and gentlemen," Daddy said, removing his top hat with a flourish, "because the closer you watch, the less you see!"

A fluffy white bunny leaped out of the hat. The audience applauded. Several of the Red Cross girls said, "Oooh, look at the precious little bunny rabbit!"

Daddy put the precious bunny rabbit back into the top hat. "Abracadabra!" Daddy said. The hat was empty! More applause.

"And now!" Daddy said. He motioned to Mother. Mother, in tights and spangles, handed him his wand. A roll on the drums. Daddy waved his wand over the empty hat. "Abracadabra!" Daddy said, and pulled a rabbit out of the hat.

The fact that the rabbit had gained ten pounds, lost an ear, and dyed itself brown during its magical disappearance didn't bother the G.I. audience one bit.

"More! More!" they shouted, stamping their feet. They whistled. They applauded. "More!"

G.I.s put up with a lot during World War II.

Once more back home in Great Neck, Long Island, after one of these U.S.O. tours, Mother would unpack the suitcases and put the rabbits back into their permanent hutches. Then she would restore the doves used in the act to their cages and the goldfish to their bowls and feed everybody, including Daddy, Joyce and me.

After that she went over the household bills, ironed some sheets, vacuumed the living room, crocheted somebody a muffler, and committed to memory a list of fifty items for a new mind-reading code.

After that, she went to bed.

No wonder with such a mother I was skeptical about the guaranteed love spell when my friend Lorna told me about it. I said, "Really, Lorna, I'm surprised at you. Love spells! Honestly."

Lorna pointed out to me that the spell had been cast successfully a number of times in neighboring Danbury (Danbury, Connecticut. Founded 1756. Burned by British troops under General Tryon in 1777. Later rebuilt, after a fashion).

"A love spell that will work in Danbury," Lorna said, "is bound to work anyplace."

I had to agree.

"My cleaning lady gave me the spell," Lorna said. "She's from Haiti and she got it from a Haitian voodoo priest. Just to prove how well it works she cast it on one of the package boys at the Danbury A and P and now she can't get rid of him. He's infatuated. He telephones her twice a day. He sends her roses. She's at her wit's end."

Lorna also revealed that she had loaned the spell to Betty Sue Beasley, also in Danbury. Betty Sue Beasley is extremely plain-looking and has never to my knowledge had a date in her life.

"Betty Sue Beasley," Lorna informed me, "is now engaged to be married to a wealthy young hat manufacturer, also from Danbury."

"I don't believe it," I said.

"Not only is she engaged," Lorna said, "but he is taking Betty Sue on a honeymoon trip around the world on the S.S. *Rotterdam*. He gave her a diamond engagement ring the size of a pigeon's egg. *And* he told me that he thinks Betty Sue Beasley is the most enchanting, exciting, and fascinating female he has ever known in his life."

So in case anyone out there is interested, here is the spell.

### Love Spell

Purchase a candle. This candle must be brand new and purchased for the sole purpose of casting the spell. Do not utter a single word to anyone while en route to purchase the candle. If a word is spoken the spell will not work, remember. Tie a black thread around the candle. Turn the candle upside down. At midnight light the candle. While it burns recite aloud the following incantation:

"I bring you a betel leaf to chew upon, Prince Ferocious.

Hear me, oh (*name of person on whom spell is being cast*)

And at sunrise long only for me.

Hear me, oh (*name of person on whom spell is being cast*)

And at sunset long only for me.

Let (*name of person on whom spell is being cast*) neither eat nor drink because of love for me

Let (*name of person on whom spell is being cast*) neither rest nor sleep because of love for me

Let (*name of person on whom spell is being cast*) desire me night and day

And let him follow me forever as the sun follows the moon."

Clap hands together three times and blow the candle out.

That's it.

I haven't actually cast it myself yet. Lorna's cleaning lady doesn't seem to have brought along from the voodoo priest any directions for uncasting it, and it looks pretty powerful to me. I can't help thinking about the Danbury A and P package boy.

Also I want to make absolutely certain that when I eventually do cast the spell I am casting it on Mr. Right.

What if I made a mistake and instead of casting it on (*name of person on whom spell is being cast*) I accidentally cast it on Buffalo Bill or President Taft or Harry Houdini himself?

Even a voodoo priest won't be able to get me out of a mess like that.

# 9

# *Bah. Humbug.*

"Once upon a time," Charles Dickens wrote in *A Christmas Carol*, "of all the good days of the year, on Christmas Eve—old Scrooge sat busy in his counting-house."

If old Scrooge had been a retail florist, it might have explained a good deal about his personality.

There is a small flower shop over on the East Side of New York where the owner hangs a special sign over his corsage counter at Christmastime. This sign does not say "Merry Christmas" and it does not say "Season's Greetings" either. The sign says "Don't Ask for a Nice Corsage!"

I worked as a salesgirl in the family flower shop every Christmas of my life. So did all the other female members of the family. If your family happens to own a flower shop—no matter where the shop is located, no matter if it is large or small, prosperous or failing, no matter what—you work in it at Christmas. The only acceptable excuse for not showing up is if you are in active childbirth.

Daddy's shop, known as Trepel Rockefeller Center, was located in the heart of Radio City at the corner of Fifth Av-

enue and Forty-ninth Street, directly across from Saks
Fifth Avenue and St. Patrick's Cathedral.

Vanderbilts and Whitneys streamed through the doors
of Trepel Rockefeller Center at the Christmas season to
mingle with Broadway producers, European opera stars,
N.B.C. executives, Catholic bishops, prominent newscast-
ers, and Arabian oil potentates, all of them crying, as in
one voice, for a nice corsage.

"It was cold, bleak, biting weather that Christmas Eve,"
Dickens wrote, "foggy withal. The City clocks had only
just gone three, but it was quite dark already: it had not
been light all day."

Christmas Eve. Outside the windows of Trepel's the
snowflakes are falling. Lights shine through the fog from
every office building. Salvation Army Santas in woolen
whiskers and red flannel suits call "Ho-ho-ho!" and jingle
their bells. Saks Fifth Avenue's windows glitter and gleam
with Christmas treasure. Choir boys shivering in their scarlet cassocks bravely sing glad carols in the frosty air.

Inside Trepel's, Daddy is waiting on a very important
customer.

"I can't decide whether to send Mother a red or a white
poinsettia this year, Jack," the very important customer is
saying. He lights up an important cigar and goes on, "I sent
a red last year. But I don't know—maybe white would be
nice for a change."

Poinsettia plants are the florist's favorite at Christmas
because they are already potted, they are easy to handle,
and they are ready for delivery without further fuss, unlike
flower arrangements which must each be painstakingly de-
signed and made up and individually wrapped and pack-
aged.

"We could send a white poinsettia this year," Daddy says to the important customer. He does his best to give the impression that whether customer's mother gets a red or a white poinsettia is the question closest to his heart at this joyous season. "We could put a red bow on it," Daddy says.

Daddy, like his employees, has by this time been on his feet for three days and nights straight, with only an occasional catnap snatched on a cot in the back room.

He has also been dealing with the usual avalanche of holiday disasters ranging from dead Christmas trees in the Radio City Music Hall lobby to a rush order for seventy-five nice corsages that has just been phoned in by an N.B.C. vice-president.

"Wernher von Braun is on the telephone from Huntsville, Alabama, Jack," Mother says. Mother is handling the out-of-town telephone orders this Christmas. "Do we have any nice long-stemmed roses, he wants to know?"

"Beautiful roses," Daddy says, and turning back to the important customer he asks, "Would you like us to pick out the poinsettia for you, sir?"

"Hold it a minute, Jack," the customer says. "What's that fancy-looking thing over there?"

"It's a holiday table centerpiece arrangement," Daddy says, stifling a groan. Daddy knows already what is coming next.

"It's a beauty," the customer says. "Forget the poinsettia plant. Send Mother one of those table centerpiece doodads instead."

This is an example of what is known among retail florists as Scrooge's Law. Scrooge's Law states, roughly, that if a customer is able to order something complicated and difficult at Christmas rather than something simple and easy, the customer will do so.

A traffic cop comes into the shop and says loudly, "Either you guys move your delivery truck within the next two minutes or it gets towed away and if that smart-ass driver gives me any more of his lip I'll bust him in the chops!"

"Joy to the world, the Lord is come!" the cathedral choir boys sing.

"I want the table arrangement up at Mother's apartment on Ninetieth Street pronto, Jack," the important customer tells Daddy.

"We'll try," Daddy says. The arrangement, Daddy knows, is going to require the labor of his top designer for almost an hour, after which it will have to be carefully swathed in tissue paper, wrapped, boxed, loaded on to the truck (provided the truck has not by that time been towed away by the New York City Police Department), and delivered to an address forty blocks north of Rockefeller Center.

"We'll do our best," Daddy tells the customer.

"Best is not good enough," customer says, lighting up another big cigar. "I want it up there *pronto!* Otherwise I'll go over to Max Schling's on Madison Avenue and order something from *his* shop."

"I'm sorry to interrupt you, Jack dear," Aunt Anna says, interrupting Daddy and the important customer, "but I have just been spoken to very rudely by your porter who is sweeping the floor."

Aunt Anna, in the family tradition, shows up at the shop each Christmas, much to everybody's annoyance, because she talks incessantly about how rich she is.

"I am here only to help my brother Jack," she tells everybody. "I refuse to accept one penny of salary. I don't need the money and I don't want it and I won't accept it. All I ask is a little gratitude."

She also eats a lot of free sandwiches, writes delivery

tags in an illegible handwriting, and gives herself expensive free corsages which she wears upside down.

"This very rude, coarse porter," Aunt Anna tells Daddy, going on with her story, "said to me in a very rude and coarse tone of voice, 'Lady, move those feet of yours out of my way!' I want you to discharge him at once."

"Love and joy come to you and to you glad Christmas too!" the choir boys sing.

"Please, can I buy a nice corsage for my mommy?" a small child says, coming into the shop with a dime clutched in his mittened hand.

Daddy has given standing orders that any child wishing to buy flowers for Mommy is to be treated as a bona-fide customer, regardless of how small an amount of money the child has.

"May I help you?" I say to the mittened child. I serve Trepel's at Christmas as the last and weakest link in the waiting-on-customers chain of command and, unless an emergency arises, am restricted to waiting only on small impoverished children, office-party revelers, and tourists who wish to purchase one of our fifty-cent, four-leaf-clover key chains.

"My mommy likes pink roses," the child tells me.

I sell the child a corsage of pink sweetheart roses for a dime.

"What is this?" Uncle Ingomar demands, eying the dime with suspicion. Uncle Ingomar is tending the cash register.

"It's a dime," I tell him.

"You must have made an error of some sort," Uncle Ingomar says. "Nothing in this shop sells for a dime. The cheapest item we carry is our four-leaf-clover key chain, which sells for fifty cents."

"The dime is for a corsage of pink sweetheart roses I just sold to a small child," I say.

"A corsage of pink sweetheart roses costs this shop five dollars," Uncle Ingomar says. "This includes the cost of the flowers themselves, the cost of the labor, the cost of the fern, the cost of the ribbon, the cost of the box, and the cost of two corsage pins. By selling a corsage of pink sweetheart roses for a dime you have incurred a loss of four dollars and ninety cents."

"The corsage was for the small child's mommy," I say.

"Bah!" said Scrooge. "Humbug!"

"I have an F.T.D. order on the phone from Ohio," Mother tells the manager of Trepel's. "Ohio wants a nice five-dollar poinsettia for delivery uptown."

F.T.D. stands for Florists' Telegraph Delivery, a world-wide organization of florists, which makes it possible for somebody in Ohio to exclaim suddenly, on Christmas Eve, "Holy catfish, I've forgotten to send Cousin Frederica in New York anything for Christmas!"

Somebody in Ohio then instructs his local florist, in a panic, to immediately send a poinsettia to Cousin Frederica with a card reading "Merry Christmas from Nephew Ted." "Something nice for around five dollars," somebody in Ohio adds.

Ohio now telephones Trepel's and says, "We have an order for you—poinsettia plant card to read 'Merry Christmas from Nephew Ted'—something nice for five dollars."

Trepel's manager takes the phone from Mother and says into it, "We sold the last five-dollar poinsettia days ago, Ohio. There's not a five-dollar poinsettia plant available in the whole city of New York."

"Well, do the best you can," Ohio says cheerfully. "And a merry Christmas to all you folks out there in the big town."

So Trepel's delivers its least-expensive poinsettia plant (ten dollars) all the way uptown to Cousin Frederica by special messenger (three dollars) who has to take a taxi (two dollars) because there is a bus strike on for Christmas in New York City.

And not only that but the day after Christmas Cousin Frederica is going to descend on Trepel's in a rage and say, "I have never seen such a tiny little poinsettia plant in all my life and I know my nephew Ted, he is a big spender and would never order a dinky plant like that and I have a good mind to call the Better Business Bureau and tell them what a bunch of cheats you florists are!"

"There's another fellow," Scrooge said, "talking about a merry Christmas. I'll retire to Bedlam."

"Hey, babe, did you write out this address tag?" Hymie the delivery-truck driver asks Aunt Anna. Hymie belongs to the teamsters' union, which does not recognize Aunt Anna as a bargaining agent.

"Yes I wrote it, why do you ask, may I inquire?" Aunt Anna replies frostily.

"Well, kid, you must of been bombed when you did," Hymie says. "There ain't no such address as North Eighty-ninth Avenue, and if there was it would be six feet under the Hudson River."

"Oh holy night, the stars are brightly shining," the choir boys sing. This is their last carol. They are getting ready to go home. It is Christmas Eve and everyone is going home because nobody works on Christmas Eve except ushers, waiters, bus drivers, policemen, nurses, pilots, firemen, conductors, telephone operators, radio announcers, stewardesses, control-tower operators, actors, florists, and Santa Claus.

"Your delivery-truck driver has spoken very rudely to me, Jack," Aunt Anna tells Daddy.

"Here's the table centerpiece for that important customer's mother," the head designer tells Daddy.

"Forget the centerpiece," the manager tells Daddy. "The customer just phoned and canceled the order. He wants us to send his mother a poinsettia instead."

"There isn't a poinsettia left in the shop," the plant buyer tells Daddy. "There isn't a poinsettia to be had in all of New York."

Aunt Anna begins to eat another tunafish salad sandwich. She is wearing a free orchid corsage on her dress.

"Your corsage is upside down, Aunt Anna," I tell her. "Flowers are supposed to be worn the way they grow with the petals pointing upwards."

"Well!" Aunt Anna says. "The nerve of some people!" She puts on her hat.

"Your daughter has just spoken to me very rudely," she tells Daddy and goes home to change her will. Uncle Ingomar locks up the cash register and goes home to help her.

"Sleep in heavenly peace!" the cathedral choir boys sing, and they go home to dream of sugar-plum fairies.

Perry Como telephones from California and asks for a poinsettia plant to be delivered as soon as possible to an elderly aunt on Central Park South. Daddy gets on the phone and says, "Why don't you let us send her a nice corsage instead, Mr. Como?"

"Well, okay, as long as it's nice," Perry Como says.

"It will be nice," Daddy says.

"It was always said of him," Dickens wrote, "that he knew how to keep Christmas well, if any man alive possessed the knowledge. May that be truly said of us, and all of us! And so, as Tiny Tim observed, God Bless Us, Every One!"

# 10

# Love and Sex and All That Nonsense

Mother taught me while I was growing up that if I fell in love with Mr. Right and married him and stayed home and dusted and mopped and baked blueberry muffins, I would live happily ever after.

"That's what happened to me when I met your wonderful father," she told me. "And, incidentally, try to remember that it's just as easy to fall in love with a rich man as with a poor man."

She was 100 per cent right and I wish I had listened to her. She also told me that if I didn't practice the piano I would be sorry when I grew up. I *am* sorry, too.

Instead of marrying Mr. Right I married what turned out to be Mr. Wrong, and he wasn't rich, either, and one day I woke up and found myself the first member of the family to be divorced.

It happened like this: I was bustling around the house dusting and mopping and humming happy little tunes

when I happened to look around, and my husband was
gone.

"George?" I said. "George? Where are you, George?"

It turned out where George was, was with a friend of
mine whom I will call Gloria. Boy, do I still hate that
Gloria! Gloria's house was teeming with dust and Gloria
didn't know which end of a mop was which.

"She's gorgeous," I sobbed to Mother. "She has red hair
and translucent skin. George is in love with her. He wants
me to give him a divorce." I hiccuped. "I'll never dust
again, that I'll tell you!" I informed Mother.

Besides having red hair and translucent skin, Gloria had
a husband and three children but that didn't seem to
bother her. It didn't bother George either. He wanted me
to give him a divorce immediately, preferably within the
next ten minutes.

"No," I said. "I love you. I will not divorce you."

My theory, founded by the editors of the *Ladies' Home
Journal* and reinforced by Hollywood was that if I hung on
long enough everything would turn out fine, the way it
turns out in the movies when Greer Garson's wandering
husband sees the error of his ways and returns home to
bravely smiling Greer Garson.

Nothing turned out that way. "I want a divorce," George
said again.

"But I love you, George!" I said, baking a few blueberry
muffins just in case. I had switched over from being a good
sport like Greer Garson to being a good sport like June
Allyson where, even though her legs have been amputated
at the hip, she never complains.

"I want a divorce," George said. "Damn it."

Love in real life, I concluded, is not like love is in the
movies and the *Ladies' Home Journal*. Love in real life
tends to be crumby.

"You win," I told George. "I'll go down to Alabama and you can have your divorce and I hope you both choke on it!" I had given up good sportsmanship along with dusting. "I'll never forgive either of you as long as I live," I said.

I got on a plane for Huntsville, Alabama. Back in those days one could get an Alabama divorce by registering at an Alabama hotel, filing for a divorce in the morning, and returning back home that afternoon. Alabama kindly mailed the decree up north a few days later.

"It's all over," I told Mother. "The divorce is final. George married Gloria yesterday."

"Good riddance to him," Mother said.

A psychiatrist wrote me a letter once after reading one of my books. In the letter he said it was obvious from my writing that my mother had implanted in me a bunch of unrealistic, romantic notions about marriage. Therefore, the psychiatrist said, my divorce was basically my mother's fault.

"Don't blame yourself, Mrs. Kampen," the letter ended. "Blame your mother."

I didn't bother to write back and argue with the psychiatrist. It wouldn't have done any good. Psychiatrists have discovered that everything that goes wrong in this world can eventually be traced to the fault of somebody's mother.

Whatever a mother does, it is a bad thing. If it turns out by some accident to be a good thing, nobody remembers it.

Take sex education. Mother's generation didn't believe in it.

"There's no point wasting a lot of valuable time worrying about love and sex and all that nonsense," Mother said briskly. "Never let a boy lay a hand on you. Keep that in mind and you won't get into trouble."

She was absolutely right, too, just the way she was right about practicing the piano, and I only wish I had listened to her. Instead I listened to Cookie O'Gorsky. Cookie was a year older than I was and lived across the street from us in Brooklyn.

"You know what I can't stand about Cookie O'Gorsky?" my sister, Joyce, once said to me. "I can't stand that she knows everything."

Cookie didn't really know everything but she acted as if she did, which back in Brooklyn amounted to the same thing.

Cookie had a younger sister named Odette. When Odette was six years old she had a fight with Cookie and she decided to teach her older sister a lesson by committing suicide.

"I hate you!" Odette shouted at Cookie. "I'm going to throw myself into the ocean. Good-bye forever, you mean thing!"

And Odette rushed out of the O'Gorsky house and headed for nearby Sheepshead Bay to jump off the Sheepshead Bay bridge. Cookie ran out of the house after her.

"Take your sweater," Cookie said to Odette. "Mama will be mad if you catch cold when you jump without a sweater."

That was Cookie O'Gorsky, who taught me all I know about sex. I don't know who taught Cookie about sex. Most of what she handed on to me turned out to be wrong—not only wrong but wrong in a spectacular and baroque fashion.

"All boys," Cookie confided in me, "have three you-know-whats."

I had never seen a nude male and Cookie had—she claimed to have in her possession a snapshot of Bernie Zitzmann, a boy who lived on the next block and went to Poly

Prep, without any clothes on—so I took her word for the three you-know-whats.

"If a girl talks to a stranger in the ladies' room of Grand Central Station that girl will be drugged by the white slavers and end up in a cage in Hong Kong," Cookie told me.

"If a girl allows a boy to give her a deep soul kiss that girl will probably become pregnant and give birth to a colored child," Cookie told me.

"A girl can have a baby," Cookie went on, "even if she never lets a boy lay a hand on her." I demanded to know how. "By taking a bath in the same bathtub after a boy did you-know-what in it," Cookie said.

I didn't know what, but I was ashamed to admit it to Cookie who, whenever she got to the interesting parts about sex, switched to the euphemism "you-know-what."

"No, I do not know what," I would admit once in a great while, my mortification at not knowing what overcome by my morbid curiosity. "What?"

"*That*," Cookie would reply. "Certainly you know what *that* is. Everybody knows."*

At this point I usually backed down and answered weakly, "Oh sure, I know what *that* is. I thought you meant something else," and was left as much in the dark as ever as to what you-know-what was or, in the case of Bernie Zitzmann, what three you-know-whats were.

I saw Cookie O'Gorsky when I was out in California a couple of years ago. We met for a reunion lunch in the Polo Lounge of the Beverly Hills Hotel. Cookie lives in Los Angeles.

"The Polo Lounge is actually the only important place in town to lunch," Cookie told me. "All the movie stars eat here."

* See Chapter entitled "Ah Jus' Love Readin', Doan Y'All?"

We ordered cocktails. "When did you sky in from Gotham?" Cookie asked me. Cookie writes a weekly gossip column for one of the Hollywood trade papers.

"Day before yesterday," I told Cookie. "On the midnight bird," I added.

"And what are you up to these days?" Cookie wanted to know. "Are you scripting another book?"

"Trying to," I said.

"God, I wish I had the time in my busy frantic existence to sit down and write a book," Cookie said. "I envy you. What's this new book going to be about, may I ask?"

"Oh, this and that," I said. "As a matter of fact, Cookie, you're in it."

"I am?" Cookie said, wide-eyed. "How exciting! Imagine me being in a book! What do you say about me in the book?"

"I say," I told her, "that you told me wrong things about sex when we lived in Brooklyn."

Cookie put down her cocktail and said to me indignantly, "I never in my entire life told you a wrong thing about sex!"

"You did too," I said.

The Polo Lounge loudspeaker said, "Paging John Wayne. Telephone call for Mr. John Wayne."

I looked around, but Mr. Wayne was nowhere in sight.

"I challenge you to name just one wrong thing I told you about sex," Cookie said to me. "Go ahead—name one."

I thought for a moment. "You told me a wrong thing about the male anatomy," I said.

"Miss Lucille Ball wanted at the front desk," the loudspeaker said. "Miss Ball, front desk, please."

Miss Ball didn't seem to be in the Polo Lounge either.

"What did I tell you wrong about the male anatomy?" Cookie asked me.

"You said boys have three you-know-whats," I said. "You told me you had a snapshot of Bernie Zitzmann without any clothes on and that he had three you-know-whats."

"What?" Cookie said.

"You know," I said, "those."

"Oh, *those!*" Cookie said. She laughed lightly. "I was only teasing when I told you that. My heavens, Irene, you must have been naive in those days! I thought everybody in the world knew about *those*."

"Paging Shelley Winters," the loudspeaker said. "Will Miss Winters please come to the telephone?"

"I'm glad we decided to come here to the Polo Lounge for lunch," Cookie said. "It's where all the movie stars eat."

"I intend to make very certain that if I ever have a daughter she and I will feel free to discuss sex freely and frankly," I told Mother in righteous tones. Unfortunately before I could get around to discussing sex with Christine at all she came home one day from fifth grade and said Dr. Safford had told them all about everything.

"He came to school with diagrams and stuff and talked about it," Chris said. "It's interesting."

I waited for her to go on.

"When you say that Dr. Safford told you all about everything," I said, finally, "exactly what do you mean by 'everything'?"

"Oh, about boys and babies and that stuff," Chris said. "You know."

"Oh, sure, *that* stuff," I said. I waited some more and then I said, "Well, if there's anything Dr. Safford didn't tell you that you want to ask about I certainly hope you'll ask me, your mother."

"I will," Chris said.

That was back in nineteen fifty-five. Chris was ten years

old. She is now a grown-up professor at a big university and she hasn't asked me anything about sex since, so I guess Dr. Safford actually did tell the fifth grade all about everything.

I try not to dwell too much on love and sex and all that nonsense myself these days, what with pollution and the economic crisis to worry about. One question, though, nags at my mind. Suppose Cookie O'Gorsky was telling the truth long ago, back in Brooklyn, and Bernie Zitzmann did have three you-know-whats after all?

If so I'd certainly like to run into him again.

# 11

## If It's Marked Down, Grab It

In her feverish quest for bargains Mother occasionally got confused and bought back, for good money, something she had given away in the first place.

"Just look at this suitcase I bought myself at the Ridgefield Library White Elephant Sale!" she said to me. "It will be perfect to take along on my trip abroad with Cousin Barbara next month."

"But you already have a brand-new Vuitton suitcase for the trip, Mother," I said.

"It's ridiculous to carry a brand-new bag on a trip abroad," Mother told me. "The airlines are so careless handling luggage. Remember the big rip Pan-American tore in my suitcase two years ago in Athens?"

"I remember," I said, "because the same rip is right there in the suitcase you just bought for yourself at the White Elephant Sale. You have just bought back the suitcase you gave to last year's White Elephant Sale. You have just bought back the same suitcase that Pan-American ripped in Athens two years ago, for heaven's sake!"

"No wonder they only charged me three dollars for it," Mother said.

Mother also once in a while bought back and presented to me something she had given to me before, which I had subsequently given away.

"Look what I picked up for you at the Episcopal Church White Elephant Sale!" Mother said. It was the summer of 1959. "Two dozen in the box," Mother said gleefully. "Never been used, never even been unpacked. What a bargain!"

"What is it?" I said suspiciously.

"Plastic patio plates," Mother said. "They'll be ideal for when you invite friends in for a fork supper on your patio this summer."

"I have no patio," I said. Mother said I had a porch.

"A porch is not a patio, Mother," I said, "just as a house is not a home. And if I did happen to have a patio, which I don't, the chances of my inviting two dozen friends over to eat a fork supper on it, whatever a fork supper is, are remote."

"You certainly are grouchy today," Mother said. "Here I go out and pick up at a tremendous bargain two dozen plastic patio plates for you and this is the thanks I get."

"What's a patio plate?" I said. Mother opened the carton and showed me. A patio plate is a plastic molded dinner plate with indentations in it for various types of food. It is like an army mess kit, only uglier. After Mother left I stuck the carton of patio plates away in the back of a closet.

Four years later I came across it again for the first time while I was cleaning the closet. By this time I had forgotten exactly what the plates looked like. I reopened the carton.

"Ugh," I said.

I donated the plates, still in the original carton, to the Red Cross White Elephant Sale. Ridgefield conducts an endless series of White Elephant sales during which the inhabitants of Ridgefield buy and sell old things back and forth to each other, somewhat like Emerson's legendary villagers who earned a precarious living by taking in each other's washing.

Mother came over to my house the following day and said, "Remember those patio plates I gave you years ago? By a stroke of luck, really incredible, I came across two dozen identical plates at the White Elephant Sale today."

"And you bought them," I said.

"Naturally I bought them," Mother said. "For you, I mean. Now you have a full set."

"This means that I can invite forty-eight friends over for a fork supper," I said. Mother said to come out to the car and help her carry the patio plates in.

"They're still in the original carton," Mother said. "Never even been unpacked."

Along with patio plates that had never been unpacked and suitcases that had never been carried, Mother specialized in clothes that were too good to wear.

"The black dress?" Mother would say, if I suggested a certain frock for her to put on in order to attend a luncheon. "You can't mean the black dress with the fringe? The one I bought last month in Loehmann's? Why, Irene dear, that dress is much too good to wear just to a luncheon."

Loehmann's is a shop which specializes in selling expensive designer clothes at bargain prices. Most of Mother's dresses too good to wear came from Loehmann's.

"A Dior!" Mother would cry, prowling excitedly through

the Loehmann racks. "And see here—an original Scaasi! And look at this genuine Balenciaga!"

"Wonderful," I said apathetically. You had to take Mother's word about the genuine Dior and Scaasi and Balenciaga because Loehmann's removed the original labels from its dresses before putting them on sale.

"Look at this, Irene!" Mother said. She had stopped in her tracks. "Come here!" she called to me. "Hurry!" I was trailing behind her through the aisles. She now snatched an evening gown from a rack.

"I saw the identical gown advertised by Bergdorf Goodman in this morning's newspaper!" Mother told me.

"You did?" I said. I glanced surreptitiously at my wristwatch. We had been wandering around Loehmann's for what seemed to me like hours. I hated shopping in Loehmann's. My idea of shopping was to take a taxicab directly to Bergdorf Goodman's, buy myself a dress, pay for it, and if possible wear it home that same day.

"This is a genuine Mollie Parnis," Mother said in hushed tones, examining the gown she had snatched from the rack. "Look at it, Irene—it's unmistakably Mollie Parnis."

"Oh, unmistakably," I said. "Buy it, Mother, it will be perfect on you. Don't waste a minute—grab it!" Anything to get Mother out of Loehmann's and into a restaurant for lunch.

"Bergdorf's is asking two hundred dollars for this very same dress," Mother said.

"Worth every penny," I said automatically. And I added again, "Grab it."

"Oh, I don't want it for myself," Mother said. "I have a closet full of perfectly good evening gowns I've scarcely worn. I want you to buy it for you."

I now took a good look at the dress Mother was holding.

Either Mother was mistaken about it being a genuine Mollie Parnis or else Mollie had been having a bad day.

"You might have to shorten it a bit," Mother said. "Maybe if you take the orange ruffle off the bottom it won't be too long."

"I won't have to shorten it because it won't be too long because I'm not buying it," I said. "It's the worst-looking dress I've seen in a long time."

Mother didn't pay the slightest attention. She was busy examining the price tag on the genuine Mollie Parnis.

"It's absolutely hideous," I said.

"This gown," Mother informed me, "has been marked down from its original price of two hundred dollars to—are you ready?—*twenty-nine ninety-five!*"

"I know why," I said.

"Twenty-nine ninety-five for a genuine Mollie Parnis!" Mother said. "It's unbelievable."

"Let's please go have lunch, Mother," I said.

"I refuse to allow you to pass up a bargain like this one," Mother told me firmly. "If you won't buy the gown for yourself I'm going to buy it for you. Twenty-nine ninety-five! It's worth the money even if you let it hang in your closet for a year."

Mother bought the genuine Mollie Parnis for me. It hung in my closet for a year and at the end of the year I gave it, still unworn, to the Girl Scout White Elephant Sale.

The Girl Scouts marked the genuine Mollie Parnis down to five dollars and Mother bought it again.

"I took a ticket to the Firemen's Buffet Supper, but I don't know what to wear," Mother told me some time later.

"Wear the original Mollie Parnis that was marked down from two hundred dollars to five dollars," I said.

"You can't be serious," Mother said. "A dress like that—an original Mollie Parnis—is much too good to wear to a buffet supper."

Loehmann's doesn't sell fur coats so when I decided to buy myself a fur coat, Mother got the address of some furrier in New York.

"It's wholesale," Mother told me. "We're supposed to go in and ask for Eidermann."

We went in and asked for Eidermann. Eidermann brought out a coat and said to me, "Try this one on." I tried it on. "Gorgeous," Eidermann said.

"What kind of fur is this supposed to be?" Mother asked. Eidermann said it wasn't *supposed* to be, it *was*.

"All right, Eidermann, what kind of fur *is* it?" Mother said.

"Mink paws," Eidermann said. "Trimmed at the hem with hads." Mother said trimmed with what? "Hads!" Eidermann said. "Mink hads! Hads from minks!"

"Oh, *heads*," Mother said.

I studied my reflection in the mirror. "What do you think, Mother?" I said.

"It's not your coat," Mother said.

"You're right," I said. I took the coat off. Eidermann whisked it away and returned with another one.

"Try this gorgeous thing on," Eidermann said to me.

"What kind of—?" Mother began, but Eidermann forestalled her.

"Hungarian blond wolf," Eidermann said. "Imported, of course," he added.

I tried on the Hungarian blond wolf. Hungarian blond wolf is an extremely fluffy fur.

"It's gorgeous!" I said. "I want it."

"Now don't be so hasty, Irene," Mother said. "First of

all, Eidermann, a few questions. Is Hungarian wolf on the endangered animals list?"

Eidermann gave a hollow laugh.

"Packs of Hungarian wolves are raging through the Hungarian countryside killing innocent peasants," he told Mother, "and you, my dear madame, are asking me if the wolves are endangered!"

He laughed once more, bitterly, and said, "The wolves are not endangered—it is the Hungarians who are endangered!"

He fell silent, breathing heavily.

"How much is the coat?" Mother asked.

Eidermann wrenched his thoughts away from the endangered Hungarians and said, "Two thousand dollars."

"Take the coat off," Mother said to me.

"What are you rushing?" Eidermann said to Mother. "Give a person a chance to finish a sentence, Mrs. Trepel. I was about to say this coat is two thousand dollars *including* a genuine leather belt, choice of buttons, choice of lining, free storage for five years, and a three-letter monogram."

"Well . . . ," Mother said.

"Old English letters," Eidermann said.

"I'll buy it," I told Eidermann, but Mother said, "It's pretty on you, dear, but I wonder if it isn't a bit too fluffy?"

"Fluffy?" Eidermann cried. "Certainly it's fluffy! You think a Hungarian wolf should have scales like a fish? Feathers, like a chicken?" He gave Mother a look and said, again, "Fluffy! Ha!"

"Don't start with the 'Ha', Eidermann," Mother said. "Don't give me any 'Ha's, if you please."

"A person isn't even allowed to say 'Ha' nowadays in the United States?" Eidermann said. " 'Ha' is suddenly against the law?"

"This is my daughter's first fur coat and I want to be sure she's getting her money's worth," Mother said.

"This identical coat is hanging in Bergdorf's fur salon with a price tag on it of three thousand dollars!" Eidermann informed Mother. "Three thousand dollars! In Bergdorf's!"

But Mother was not about to be Bergdorfed by the likes of Eidermann. "It doesn't seem to be a hardy fur," she said.

"Hungarian wolf is the hardiest fur known to man," Eidermann told her. Mother said how about shedding? Eidermann said, "Unsheddable." Mother said what about rain?

"Rain?" Eidermann repeated. He turned to me and said, "Your mother is asking about rain. Ha!"

"Don't 'Ha' me, Eidermann," Mother said. "Just answer my question, please. Will my daughter be able to wear this coat in the rain?"

"Mrs. Trepel," Eidermann said earnestly, "one question, if you don't mind. Have you ever seen a wolf carrying an umbrella?"

Not long after Mother passed away I was on an errand in Norwalk, Connecticut. The only parking space I could find was in front of Loehmann's. In Loehmann's front window was a white floor-length ostrich feather boa.

All my life I had longed for an ostrich feather boa.

"Of all the impractical articles of clothing one could buy, Irene," I told myself, "the most impractical is a white floor-length ostrich feather boa. It is perishable. It will molt. It will shed. It is unsuitable for daytime wear. It cannot be taken along on a trip. It is too large to fit into any suitcase devised by man."

I went into Loehmann's and tried on the white floor-length ostrich feather boa. I resembled a cross between

Carol Channing and "Sesame Street's" Big Bird, but I didn't care. I wanted that boa.

"How much?" I asked the saleslady.

"Seventy-five dollars," she said, "originally. Only this morning it was marked down to thirty dollars."

A mere thirty dollars for a white floor-length ostrich feather boa! An incredible bargain! Surely somewhere up in some heavenly Loehmann's stockroom Mother was busily at work marking down the merchandise.

"I'll take it," I told the saleslady.

The boa is lying in the back of my bedroom closet where it has been lying, unworn, for a year, coiled up in its giant-size Hefty Trash Bag, the only container large enough to hold it.

When I last looked at the boa it was molting. It was also beginning to shed. I only hope that before it is completely gone I will receive an invitation to some appropriate social event to which I can wear it. A European coronation or a masked ball in Venice would be just the ticket.

Even if not, at a mere thirty dollars for a genuine ostrich feather boa it was worth every penny.

## 12

# How Not to Meet Lucille Ball

It was a boiling hot August day. I was commuting home to Connecticut from my job as a salesgirl in New York City when the New Haven Railroad came to a complete halt, no doubt due to a fallen leaf on its tracks.

The conductor said, "Passenger service has been disrupted, folks," as though we didn't know. It was the third time in a week that passenger service had been disrupted.

When you are a New Haven passenger whose service has been disrupted you get to sit in a sealed railroad car without air conditioning and think long thoughts about life.

My thoughts, on that fateful August day, ran as follows:

1 I hated my job but
2 I had to keep on working because I had no husband and
3 no money and
4 a big house in Ridgefield, Connecticut, with a big mortgage and
5 a desk full of unpaid bills and

6 a sink full of dirty dishes and
7 two Siamese cats and
8 a daughter fifteen years old and
9 things looked bad.

"The five o'clock express is broken down in front of this train," the conductor said. "Cars are backed up all the way to New York. We'll be stuck here another hour at least."

"I can't stand it," I said.

"I don't blame you," the conductor said sympathetically. New Haven passengers say "I can't stand it" or, in some cases, "I can't go on like this" fairly often.

"When I get home," I said, "providing of course that I ever do get home, I'm going to write a book."

The conductor said, "Sure you are." (New Haven Railroad passengers say "I'm going to write a book" after they have said "I can't go on like this." Once in a while instead of saying they are going to write a book they say they are going to open a gift shop in Vermont. Sometimes they say they are going to move to New Hampshire and buy a basket factory.)

"I *am* going to write a book," I told the conductor. "I really am."

I did, too. It took me a year to write it because during the time I was working on it I had to keep commuting to New York.

"You type so late into the night, Mother," Chris said. I told her I was writing a book. "How come you're writing a book?" she asked.

"I'm writing a book because I can't stand it," I said. "Also I can't go on like this."

"What's the book about?" Chris said.

"It's about how amusing it is to be divorced and to live in Connecticut with two Siamese cats and a fifteen-year-old daughter who never smiles," I said.

When I finished writing the book I told Mother, "I've written a book."

"That's nice, dear," Mother said. "What's the book about?"

"It's about two hundred pages," I said. "I don't know why I bothered to write it. I know I'll never be able to get it published."

"Of course you'll get it published," Mother said. "My goodness, just think of all the terrible books that are published every day."

"I don't know any publishers or editors or literary agents," I said gloomily. "It will never be published."

"Never mind, it will be published," Mother said.

Doubleday published my book under the title *Life Without George*.

This is how it got published: I showed the manuscript to a scenic designer named Tom to whom I was introduced at a cocktail party and Tom showed it to his dentist and the dentist showed it to his accountant and the accountant showed it to his wife's sister who knew a literary agent. The literary agent showed it to Doubleday and Doubleday published it.

So attention, beginning writers! The way to get your first book published is to be introduced at a cocktail party to a scenic designer named Tom.

After Doubleday published *Life Without George* it was translated into Dutch, issued as a paperback, converted to a series of comic books, made into a paper doll and coloring book, and manufactured as a sweatshirt. All this happened because Lucille Ball bought the book as the basis for her television series.

The series is now into its twelfth year and indicates no signs of ever coming to an end. Every time *The Lucy Show* appears on a television screen—and it appears a lot—I get a royalty check.

I love Lucy.

"What is Lucille Ball really like?" people ask me.

I have no idea because I've never met Miss Ball.

On the other hand, Miss Ball has never met me.

"I'm sure she's dying to meet you, though," Mother said. I was leaving on my first trip to California. "Telephone her when you get to the Coast," Mother said. "She'll be thrilled to hear from you."

The Beverly-Wilshire Hotel in Los Angeles had kindly provided three telephones in my quarters—one next to my bed, one on my desk, and one in the bathroom, just in case.

I picked up telephone number two and dialed the number of the West Coast branch of my agency. Ten per cent of me belongs to a great big important talent agency with offices all over the world.

"I.F.A., good morning," the agency switchboard operator said. I.F.A. stands for International Famous Associates, which in my opinion is a pretty classy name for a talent agency.

I figured that for 10 per cent I was entitled to ask I.F.A to arrange a meeting with Miss Ball.

"I'm Irene Kampen," I told the operator. "I wrote the book that the Lucille Ball television series is based upon. I would like to consult somebody about meeting Miss Ball."

"I'm sorry, Miss Kamper, but the person you wish to speak to has stepped away from his desk," the operator said. "Can he get back to you?"

"Can who get back to me?" I said. The operator said whoever it was I wished to speak to about meeting Lucille Ball. "Who is he?" I asked.

"Mr. Monwin," the operator said.

I left my number for Mr. Monwin and while I was waiting for him to get back to me I went downstairs and bought a red velvet evening gown in the Beverly-Wilshire boutique in the lobby.

The evening gown cost a hundred dollars and I needed it like I needed a third set of elbows but, after all, I told myself, this is my first trip to California and I am shortly going to meet Lucille Ball.

When I got back upstairs to my room there was a message for me to call I.F.A.

"Oh, yes, Miss Kraper," the I.F.A operator said. "I'll connect you with Mr. Monwin's secretary."

"Mr. Monwin's office," Mr. Monwin's secretary said. I explained who I was. "Oh, yes, of course, Miss Kramer," the secretary said. "We've been trying to get hold of you since last Tuesday. Mr. Monwin likes the script but wants to set up a conference to talk about the possibility of a cameo role for Paul Newman."

I got the I.F.A. switchboard operator back.

"Oh, I'm so sorry, you want the television department, of course," the operator said. "I'll connect you with Mr. Yance. One of his people will be able to help you."

"Mr. Yance's office," Mr. Yance's secretary said. I explained who I was and how I had written the book for the Lucille Ball series. Mr. Yance's secretary said of course, would I just hold for a moment while she got Mr. Yance on the wire.

"I was hoping to hear from you, Mrs. Kaman," Mr. Yance said heartily when he got on the wire. "The Chicago office said you'd be getting in touch. I'm afraid I have some disappointing news, though. Paramount wardrobe has taken over this particular problem. I did my best to talk them into changing their minds but it's hopeless. I'm afraid we'll have to cancel the entire shipment of parasols that your Kankakee factory air expressed out to us here. Sorry."

I got the I.F.A. switchboard operator back again.

"I'll put you through to Media Liaison. They'll be able to help you, I'm quite sure," the operator told me.

"Media Liaison here," Media Liaison said to me. "Mr. Monwin's office." I explained for the second time all about me and Lucille Ball.

"Oh, yes, of course, Mrs. Kenner," Mr. Monwin's office said. "I spoke to Mr. Monwin about your problem and he told me to tell you it will be impossible to arrange a meeting between you and Miss Ball."

"Why impossible?" I said. Mr. Monwin's office said impossible because Miss Ball was leaving that afternoon for the Coast. "But she's already on the Coast," I said. Mr. Monwin's office said, "*East* Coast," and hung up.

I went downstairs to the lobby again. A Universal Studio Bus Tour guide was rounding up prospective customers for his tour.

"Complete guided tour of the Universal lot for only seven bucks, folks," the guide was saying. "See the famous sets used in many motion pictures. See the dressing rooms of the stars."

I gave him seven dollars and got on the tour bus.

"I'm so excited!" the woman sitting in back of me said to her husband. "Wouldn't it be wonderful if we saw a real celebrity while we are on this tour?"

As we drove through the Universal Studios lot the guide pointed out the set that had been used for *The Hardy Family* series and the set that had been used for *High Noon* and the set that had been used for *2001: A Space Odyssey*.

"And now, ladies and gentlemen," the guide said, through his megaphone, "if you will glance to the right you will see through the windows of this bus the very dressing room that Miss Lucille Ball herself uses while filming her television series *The Lucy Show!*"

All the people on the bus murmured excitedly.

"I have seen Miss Ball many a time wave to our bus as we drive past her dressing room," the guide said. "Unfortunately today Miss Ball is not in residence as she is en route to the East Coast for a television special."

"How disappointing," the woman in back of me said to her husband. "I'd give anything to actually see Lucille Ball in person."

I got up from my seat and made my way down the aisle to the front of the bus where the guide was sitting.

"I was interested in your pointing out Lucille Ball's dressing room," I told the guide, "because I have written the book on which Miss Ball's television series *The Lucy Show* is based."

The guide looked at me. In case he hadn't quite understood I said, again, "I wrote the book that Lucille Ball uses as the basis for her television series. I wrote it. The book, I mean."

I thought he would probably pick up his megaphone and announce in excitement, "Ladies and gentlemen, believe it or not, we have aboard this very bus with us today the writer of the book on which Lucille Ball bases her television series! Gee whiz! My goodness!"

What he actually did was to give me another look—the look of a man forced to deal with crazies all day, seven days a week, fifty-two weeks a year—and say, "Lady, kindly remain seated while the bus is in motion."

I went back to my seat and said, under my breath, "Phooey on you. I belong to a big important agency named International Famous Associates with offices all over the world. So there!"

Back in Los Angeles I flounced off the bus at its first stop.

("Good riddance!" I heard the tour guide say.) I walked into the lobby of the Beverly-Wilshire to find what seemed like several thousand men in Stetson hats and cowboy boots milling around the registration desk.

"It's the Pacific Coast Lumbermen's Association convention," the elevator operator told me wearily. "I don't think I can stand it."

I ordered dinner from room service. Then I dialed Mother's number.

"Irene?" Mother said. "What's wrong?"

"Nothing is wrong," I said. "I just wanted to say hello."

"Something has happened out there in Los Angeles," Mother said. "What is it?"

"Nothing has happened," I said. "Everything is marvelous."

"Have you met Lucille Ball yet?" Mother asked.

"No," I said. "She's not in town."

"I knew by the sound of your voice that something was bothering you," Mother said.

"Nothing is bothering me," I said. "How are the cats?"

"Neither of them has eaten a morsel for three days," Mother said. "Now tell me exactly what's wrong."

"Nothing is wrong!" I said.

"Nobody calls a mother at this hour unless something is wrong," Mother said.

"It's only nine o'clock at night, for God's sake," I said.

"It's midnight here," Mother said.

"I'm sorry, Mother," I said apologetically. "I always forget the time difference between California and Connecticut."

"Try to get some sleep," Mother told me. "Try not to worry about Lucille Ball."

Two hours later I picked up bedside telephone number

one and asked for the Beverly-Wilshire night manager.

"I can't stand it," I told him.

"It's the Pacific Coast Lumbermen's Association convention," the night manager told me wearily. "They have set up their official hospitality suite in the room next to yours—room 743. There is nothing I can do about the lumbermen, madame. Eventually they will all go to sleep, I suppose."

I put on my new red velvet evening gown and a lot of false eyelashes and knocked on the door of room 743. A lumberman opened the door.

"Wow!" he said, getting a load of the gown. "The lady in red! Look who's here, boys!"

"Fry my eyeballs!" the lumbermen cried. "Come on in, sweetheart! Make yourself at home."

"You're a lumberman?" one of the lumbermen asked me. He handed me a martini.

"I am the owner of a chain of lumberyards in New England," I said, accepting the martini. "My firm is called I.F.L. which stands for International Famous Lumberyards."

"That's some classy name for a chain of lumberyards," the lumberman said. "Here, have another martini and we'll drink to I.F.L."

So I had another martini and I stayed at the lumbermen's party until 6 A.M. (9 A.M. Lucille Ball time) when the party finally broke up.

"I had a wonderful time," I told the lumbermen gratefully when I left. I felt a bit guilty about having made up that fib about my chain of lumberyards, but I knew in my heart that if I had told them the truth—about me and Lucille Ball, I mean—they would have thrown me out of their hospitality suite.

# 13

## May You Be Buried in the Earth and Bake Bagels

Mother had a number of favorite proverbs. Most of them were translated from the Yiddish and had come down via Grandma Goldstein of "A klug on Columbus" and "Gerrodahere!" fame.

Mother could understand Yiddish but not speak it. Once, though, I heard her mutter something in Yiddish at that rat Maynard as he sat lounging under a tree on Mother's front lawn at four dollars an hour.

Maynard was out of earshot but I wasn't. "What did you just say about Maynard, Mother?" I asked. Mother said it was an old Yiddish expression that Grandma Goldstein used.

"It means," Mother said, "may he be buried in the earth and bake bagels." She thought for a moment and then added, "God forbid."

Speaking of bagels:

I was pushing my shopping cart down the Baked Goods aisle of the supermarket the other day when I came upon a mother whose child was lying on the floor screaming.

"Please stop screaming, Bernadette," the mother implored. She bent over the child and said, "Mother will give you another cookie if you stop screaming. Mother promises."

I ached to tell the mother that she was wasting her breath. Bernadette was going to keep on screaming even if offered another ten cookies. Bernadette was going to keep on screaming even if her mouth was stuffed full of cookies and she was dragged out of Baked Goods through Fresh Fruits and Vegetables and into the supermarket parking lot where she would hopefully be run over by a garbage truck.

I was the mother of a screamer. I know.

"Why does Christine scream so much?" the screamer's father, my husband, asked me. "What does she want?"

"I don't know," I said. What could she possibly want that I hadn't given her? I had given her dry diapers, warm milk, delicious applesauce, stuffed bears, night lights. Nothing helped. She kept on screaming.

"Some babies scream," my mother told me. "Some babies don't scream. One day she'll stop and it will be over. Until then a mother must have glass eyes and tin ears. That's an expression your great-grandmother Goldstein used to use."

"Some babies scream," the pediatrician told me. "Some babies don't scream. We can't seem to arrive at any reasonable scientific explanation why. One day she'll stop and it will be over. Try and hang on until then."

I woke up one morning with a sense of something amiss.

I looked at the clock. Seven A.M. I sat up in bed and shook my husband violently by the shoulder.

"Wake up!" I said. "She's dead!"

He sat bolt upright. "What?" he cried. "Who's dead?"

"The baby," I said. "Our baby, Christine." I stared at him in terror. "It's the first night since she was born that she didn't wake up and scream. She's dead, I know it."

My husband leaped from the bed and rushed into the nursery. He came back a moment later.

"She's sitting on the floor and playing with her dolls," he told me. "She smiled at me and said, 'Good morning, Daddy. I love you.'"

"I guess it's over, like Mother and the pediatrician said it would be," I said.

"Chris is turning into a beautiful little thing," my husband said. "She's got the Howland eyes and nose from my side of the family."

She also had the Howland sense of humor, the Howland grace, the Howland smile, and the Howland singing voice, according to her father, leaving my side of the family with full credit for the refuses-to-eat-a-mouthful-of-baked-potato and refuses-to-use-a-handkerchief-when-she-has-the-sniffles genes.

"Daddy, if the world is round how come the people who live on the bottom don't fall off?" Chris asked. She was about four at the time.

"This child is already exhibiting the Howland gift for scientific inquiry," her father said to me. "Since the original John Howland first came over to this country on the *Mayflower* every generation of Howlands has produced its quota of scientists and mathematicians."

He turned to Chris and said, "Come sit on my lap, sweetheart, and I will explain the law of gravity. When I have finished you will understand how come the people on the bottom of the world don't fall off."

Sweetheart perched on Daddy's lap. He explained to her the law of gravity. When he had finished, sweetheart said, with Howland winsomeness, "But, Daddy, I still don't understand. How come if the world is round the people on the bottom don't fall off?"

"Daddy will illustrate the principle of gravity for you by demonstration," my husband told her. "Run into the kitchen, precious, and bring Daddy a nice round orange."

Precious ran into the kitchen. I could hear her rummaging around.

"Chris is unusually alert mentally for her age," my husband said to me. "She reminds me very much of mother's cousin Augusta Howland. Brilliant woman."

Precious returned from her errand to the kitchen.

"I couldn't find an orange, Daddy," she said. "Here's a banana instead."

Precious eventually grew up to win a Ph.D. degree from the University of Wisconsin for a doctoral thesis entitled *Cold-Sensitive Mutants of Escherichia Coli Defective in Ribosome Assembly.*

What are you going to do with a kid like that?

While Chris was growing up we lived next door to a family named Schlessinger.

"I can no longer stand living next door to Sidelle Schlessinger," I told my mother. Sidelle, nicknamed Susu, was the same age as Chris. Susu Schlessinger was known throughout the neighborhood as the Perfect Child.

"Chris refuses to eat a mouthful of baked potato," I told Mother. "Susu cleans her plate at every meal. Chris refuses to take an afternoon nap. Susu sleeps like an angel every day from one to two o'clock. Chris pushed Susu into a mud puddle because Susu wanted to play with Chris's blocks. Susu gave her favorite doll to Chris for a present. Susu shares everything."

"Maybe some of this perfection will rub off on Chris," Mother said. "If you lie down with dogs you get up with fleas. That's an old expression Grandma Goldstein used to use."

"Susu's hair is naturally curly," I told Mother. "If Susu's mother tells me once more that Susu's hair is naturally curly I'll scream. Why can't just once I have something to be superior to Susu's mother about? Why can't *Chris's* hair be naturally curly?"

"Forget it," Mother said. "From snow you can't make cheesecake."

Susu had been born via natural childbirth.

"The delivery room nurses told me I was the bravest little mother they ever saw," Mrs. Schlessinger told me.

The delivery room nurses had elected me Mrs. Cowardly Custard of 1945.

"I refused to take a whiff of anesthetic," Mrs. Schlessinger went on. "I wanted to be wide-awake and alert for every thrilling moment of Susu's birth. I do think delivering a child is a woman's most meaningful experience, don't you agree?"

"Well, it's meaningful, all right," I said.

"Doctor allowed hubby Baird to be right there in the delivery room with me throughout the entire experience," Mrs. Schlessinger said.

As far as I was concerned the thought of Baird Schlessinger in a hospital gown watching the Perfect Child being born was enough to turn a person against love and sex and all that nonsense for life, but I murmured, "How nice."

"Susu wasn't all red and wrinkled at birth the way most

newborns are," Mrs. Schlessinger said. "She was as plump and pink and white and perfect as a baby doll."

Susu Schlessinger was on personal relations with God.

"Susu says God is everywhere," Chris reported to me. "She says she saw a corner of Him in my sandbox this morning."

I said it was possible that Susu Schlessinger had seen a corner of God in Chris's sandbox.

"Susu wants to know how come my daddy paints all those pictures of naked ladies without any clothes on," Chris said. "Susu says it's a sin and God doesn't like it."

"You tell Susu Schlessinger," I said to Chris, "that your daddy is a student at the Art Students League in New York City and that what he is painting has nothing to do with naked ladies, as such. Daddy is merely painting the effect of light and shadow on the human body."

This was a direct quote from Daddy. The subject of Daddy's paintings had come up recently in a discussion between Mother and me.

"How come he paints all those pictures of women without any clothes on?" my mother asked me. "Frankly, darling, if I were you I would be nervous about those paintings he does."

I reported the conversation to my husband.

"You may inform your mother," my husband said, "that I am studying to be an illustrator and one of the prerequisites of illustration is the ability to paint the effect of light and shadow on the human body. The paintings have nothing to do with nude women, as such."

I dutifully relayed this information back to my mother. My mother said, "Yes, well, mark my words. When there's a strong wind the garbage flies high."

"You're a dear to take Susu overnight," Mrs. Schlessinger said to me. The Schlessingers were going away for the weekend. "She won't be a bit of trouble, I promise you. She's perfectly behaved and she eats anything you give her."

"Wonderful," I said.

"And she goes to sleep the minute her curly little head hits the pillow," Mrs. Schlessinger said.

"Isn't that nice," I said.

"When I told her she was spending the night at Christine's house she was delighted," Mrs. Schlessinger said. "Do you know what she said when I told her?"

"No, what did she say?" I said.

"She said, 'I love Christine even if she pushed me into a nasty dirty mud puddle, Mommy,'" Mrs. Schlessinger said. "Isn't that sweet?"

"Adorable," I said.

"Chris is feeling all right, isn't she?" Mrs. Schlessinger asked. "I thought she looked a trifle pale this morning when I saw her."

"She's fine," I said.

"I suppose I imagined it," Mrs. Schlessinger laughed. "Susu's color is so rosy that I'm afraid I make unfair comparisons. 'A mother should have glass eyes,' my own mother used to tell me."

"I've heard my mother use that expression too," I said.

"We'll drop Susu at your house before we leave this evening," Mrs. Schlessinger said. "I'll give her her supper first."

Susu was dropped along with her pajamas, her toothbrush, and her security blanket.

"Where's your husband?" Susu asked me, right off the bat. "Is he upstairs painting naked ladies?"

"He's not here," I said. "Chris is in bed already. Would

you like a nice cup of hot cocoa before I tuck you both in for the night?"

"I hate cocoa," Susu said. "If I have to drink cocoa I'll vomit on your rug. I want a pastrami sandwich and three pickles."

"You're not going to get a pastrami sandwich and you're not going to get a pickle, Susu dear," I said. "You're going to get cocoa or nothing."

"I hate you," Susu told me. She aimed a kick at the cat, who happened to be passing. "I hate your pussycat too," Susu said.

"That's not very nice, Susu dear," I said. "We shouldn't kick animals. How would you like it if I came over to your house and kicked your pet turtle?"

"You couldn't," Susu said. "My turtle died yesterday. Mama put him into the garbage disposal and it quelched him away."

"I'm sorry your turtle died, Susu," I said. "Now let's go upstairs and get into our jammies and I'll read you and Chris a nice bedtime story."

"It went *quelch quelch quelch*," Susu said, giving a realistic imitation of a turtle being quelched by a garbage disposal. "*Quelch quelch quelch.*"

"That will do, Susu," I said.

"Quelch!" Susu said. I frowned at her. "Quelch," she said.

"That will do, Susu," I said again, firmly. "Go upstairs and get into your jammies. When you're ready for bed, call me."

Susu went upstairs. The telephone rang. It was Susu's mother.

"I forgot to warn you," Susu's mother told me, "that Susu may be a teeny bit sad this evening. Usually she's such a merry little thing that I was afraid you might be worried if she doesn't smile and laugh as much as usual. It's because of Sheldon."

"Who's Sheldon?" I said.

"Sheldon is Susu's pet turtle," Mrs. Schlessinger said. "Alas, not is—*was*. Sheldon passed away yesterday."

"Yes, I heard," I said. "I'm awfully sorry."

"Susu's little heart is broken," Mrs. Schlessinger said. "She was so attached to Sheldon. If she seems a trifle melancholy you *will* understand, won't you?"

"Oh, I will," I said.

"It's the *tristesse de le tortue*, to coin an expression," Mrs. Schlessinger said. "'Sadness of the turtle,' you know. Well, good night."

I hung up.

"We're ready for bed, Mommy," Chris called from her room.

I perched on the side of the bed. "What bedtime story would you girls like to hear?" I asked.

"'Goldilocks and the Three Bears,'" Susu said.

"Okay," I said. I began. "Once upon a time there were three bears. There was papa bear and mama bear and baby bear. They lived in a dear little house in the middle of the forest."

"Quelch!" Susu said. I ignored her.

"One day the three bears went for a walk in the forest," I went on, "and while they were gone a very strange thing happened."

"Quelch!" Susu said.

"Susu!" I said. I waited a moment, and then I went on. "A very strange thing happened while they were walking in the forest."

"Quelch quelch quelch quelch quelch quelch quelch!" Susu said. Chris giggled.

I stood up. "If you prefer to act like a silly little baby,

Susu," I said, "instead of listening to a lovely bedtime story, I shall say good night."

"I won't act silly any more, I promise," Susu said.

"She won't act silly any more, Mommy," Chris told me. "Tell the rest of the story."

I sat down again. "A little girl named Goldilocks came skipping through the woods," I said. "She went into the dear little house and saw three bowls of porridge on the table. She tasted the porridge in the first bowl and said, 'My, but this porridge is hot!'"

"Quelch!" Susu said.

"That does it," I said. "Good night, girls."

I closed the bedroom door behind me. "Enough is enough," I said. "Old Yiddish expression meaning it's time for a drink."

I went to the liquor cabinet and got out a bottle of gin.

"My Sunday-school teacher told us that gin rots away a person's brain," Susu said. She was standing behind me, clutching her security blanket.

"Your Sunday-school teacher is quite right, Susu," I said. "Furthermore, Susu, I hope that when I am a shut-in down at the funny farm both you and your Sunday-school teacher will find the time to drop by and pay me a Sunshine Visit."

"My mommy says gin rots away a person's brain too," Susu said. I took her by the hand and led her upstairs once more. "My daddy says gin rots away a person's brain too," Susu said. I tucked her in.

"My grandma told me gin rots away a person's brain too," Susu said.

"Good night, Susu," I said gently.

All that was many years ago. Susu grew up to marry the perfect man, according to her mother, and now Susu and her husband live in Greenwich, Connecticut, the perfect place.

I sometimes think of Susu, though, when twilight falls and I arise from my typewriter at last and get out the ice cubes and the vermouth and the gin and mix my first martini. I think of Susu, and a dismal pall casts itself over my cocktail hour. Could she have been right after all, I ask myself, as I measure out the ingredients with a trembling hand? Is it possible that she was telling the truth on that long-ago evening in my kitchen? *Does* gin rot away a person's brain?

A klug on you, Susu Schlessinger, you Perfect Child, you! May you be buried in the earth and bake bagels.

## 14

# Ah Jus' Love Readin', Doan Y'All?

I was moping around the bedroom in Brooklyn one day, recovering from some adolescent ailment, when Mother came in and handed me a book.

"See how you like this," she said. "I read them all when I was a girl. They're packed away in a box up in the attic if you want to read any more of them."

Mother went out, closing the bedroom door behind her. I sighed. It was so difficult for one to live in Brooklyn, I told myself, and be handed books to read when what one longed for was life. Life!

I sighed again and opened the book Mother had handed me. Listlessly I examined the title—*The Little Colonel's House Party* by Annie Fellows Johnston. I turned the page and read:

### Chapter One
Down the long avenue that led from the house to the great entrance gate came the Little Colonel on her pony, Tarbaby. She was dressed all in white this

May morning except for the little Napoleon hat of black velvet, set jauntily over her short light hair.

I read on, entranced. About five hours later I came to the words "The End." I got out of bed and went upstairs to the attic in a daze and pulled the next volume of the series— *The Little Colonel at Boarding School*—out of Mother's old box of books.

I took it downstairs to my bedroom and opened it. I wasn't merely reading about Lloyd Sherman, the Little Colonel, at boarding school; I *was* the Little Colonel at boarding school.

In rapid succession that month I read through every book in the series. As the Little Colonel I went to Switzerland, I acquired a dog named Hero, I had a Christmas vacation, I traveled abroad, I took an ocean voyage, and, finally, in *The Little Colonel's Knight Comes Riding*, I got married.

A starry-eyed bride, I advanced shyly down the aisle of the church in Lloydsboro, Kentucky, on the arm of my crotchety old grandfather, the Old Colonel, who adored me.

My fiancé was waiting for me at the altar, gazing at me also adoringly.

"How the people of the Valley poured into the church to wish them joy!" I read breathlessly. My wedding! I was getting married, actually getting married, to the handsomest boy in Lloydsboro! "Old and young, rich and poor, white and black," I read, "heartfelt good wishes were uttered in their 'God bless you, Miss Lloyd honey'" [the servants had always adored me, of course, just as Grandfather adored me] "as the Little Colonel, her wedding gown trailing behind her like a pure-white cloud woven on some fairy loom. . . ."

"Mama says if you don't come down to the dining room

this minute and eat dinner with the rest of us you won't get any dessert," my little sister, Joyce, said from the bedroom doorway.

"Go away," I told Joyce dreamily. "Go away, dear little sister. Deah sistah, go 'way. Ah'm bein' married."

The transformation had been completed. The middle-class environs of Brooklyn, my native home, had faded like some dull dream. In place of the red brick house on Oriental Boulevard across the street from the Manhattan Beach Baths there now stood a graceful white-columned Southern mansion.

"Mah home!" I said lovingly, drifting into the spacious drawing room at dusk to light the candles. It was my pleasant household chore to light the candles each day as dusk fell in Kentucky. "Mah harp!" I said. I paused at the exquisitely wrought golden harp in front of the drawing room bay window—the harp that had been a gift for me on my fifteenth birthday from the Old Colonel.

"Mah heart at thy sweet voice . . ." I sang lightly under my breath. I had a lovely singing voice. "Oh dahlin' buds of May!" I sang, plucking at the harp strings. I played the harp with effortless grace. "Ah wish Ah was in the land o' cotton!" I sang.

In the cold light of reality the only thing Lloyd Sherman and I had in common outside of our both being American citizens was that we each possessed crotchety old grandfathers.

The Little Colonel's grandfather, as I have mentioned before, adored me. I mean "her." She could twist the Old Colonel around her little finger.

"Doan be so cross-lookin', Grandfathah deah," the Little Colonel would tease winsomely. The Old Colonel's granite face would soften into an adoring smile as he gazed at his fair-haired blue-eyed granddaughter.

The Little Colonel's grandfather dressed always in fault-less white linen and was a distinguished Southern barrister. My grandfather wore a sable-lined overcoat, summer and winter, and spoke no English. He also scowled a lot.

"Doan be so cross-lookin', Grandfathah Trepel," I would coax winsomely, wagging a finger at him. "Deah, dahlin' Grandfathah, Ah jus' *know* you can smile a big-gah smile than that!"

Grandfathah Trepel told my mother, in Yiddish, that he suspected there was something seriously wrong with my brain. In his opinion, Grandfathah said, I ought to be sent away to some quiet place to rest for a while.

"Grandpa thinks you're crazy," my sister, Joyce, in-formed me. We were at the dinner table, candles flickering in the Kentucky dusk, the servants padding about quietly in the kitchen quarters beyond the dining room. "Grandpa told Mama you go around talking to yourself like a crazy person."

I stamped my dainty Southern foot and said to my mother, "Mothah, Ah'm tiahed of Grandfathah always complainin' about me!"

"How come your sister talks in that crazy accent?" Joyce's obnoxious little friend Odette O'Gorsky, who hap-pened to be dining with us, inquired of Joyce.

"If everybody doan stop pickin' on me Ah'm goin' to simply fall ovah in a heap on the flo!" I said.

"My sister Cookie says nobody in their crowd can stand Irene any more because she acts so stuck-up and crazy," Odette informed the rest of the table.

This was too much. I rose aristocratically and said, in a controlled and dignified manner, "Ah hope you all will ex-cuse me from this heah dinin' room."

I swept into the kitchen. Blossom Hruska, the maid, who didn't adore me, said, "It's none of my business but if you don't quit walking with your stomach stuck out in front of you like that you'll end up crippled in a wheel chair. And don't say I didn't warn you."

Cookie O'Gorsky and my other friends—"chums," Lloyd and I called our friends—were no help to me. They refused to do the charming Southern things that Lloyd's chums all did down there in Lloydsboro. They refused to ride in charabancs and have pillow fights and organize taffy pulls.

"A *taffy* pull?" my chum Cookie inquired in disbelief. "Why would I want to come over to your house for a taffy pull? I can go down to Woolworth's and buy all the taffy I want for a nickel. I think you're crazy, frankly."

My chums also declined to join me in nostalgic sing-alongs at twilight or go searching for wild strawberries in the meadow at dawn. The only activities my chums were interested in were reading *Photoplay* magazine and attending the local cinema, known vulgarly as the Itch.

My Little Colonel seizure might still be going on—providing I hadn't eventually been put away in some quiet place as Grandfathah suggested—except that Mother mercifully put an end to it by firmly repossessing all her Little Colonel books.

"Enough," Mother said. "In exchange I am hereby giving you unlimited reading rights to my collection of old Kathleen Norris novels."

Alas. Mother meant well but I fear it was a case of out of the fryin' pan into the fiah. The fiah started on the first page of Mrs. Norris's *The Story of Julia Page:*

"Julia's joyous radiant colouring was contradicted by her proud unsmiling mouth. Her eyes were dark blue, set in with a sooty finger and fringed with black thick up-curling lashes."

I put down *The Story of Julia Page* for a moment and

went to the mirror. I studied my proud unsmiling mouth. I
picked up the book again.

"Julia had the velvety tawny skin that accompanies hair
of the purest exquisite gold. The shabby frock she wore
served only to set off the glowing beauty of her com-
plexion."

I went back to the mirror to examine my shabby frock. I
didn't know it at the time, but as a Kathleen Norris heroine
I was in for a long succession of shabby frocks. Julia Page
handed her shabby frock on to Hildegarde in *Hildegarde*.
Hildegarde handed it on to young Mrs. Joccelyn in *Joccelyn's Wife*, who in turn handed it on to the beautiful
Kate Kelly in *Little Ships*. Kate returned it to Julia again
when I began to read the series for the second time
around as soon as I had finished the first.

"Leave the dishes, Mama dear," I said, as I mashed my
little velvet hat down on my golden hair. Life was a bit eas-
ier for me as Julia Page than it had been for me as Lloyd
Sherman because for one thing I was able to abandon the
Southern accent. I lived now in San Francisco, a city whose
inhabitants speak with no noticeable regional pronunciation.

"I'll tidy up the kitchen when I get back, Mama dear," I
said, glancing with fond eyes around the shabby but spotless kitchen. Several cracked plates were piled on the well-
scoured sink counter. "I want you to rest and not do any
more housework, Mama," I said. Mama was a widow.
"And don't sew in this light, Mama, it will tire your poor
eyes."

Along with the Southern accent I had been forced also
to give up the plantation. I was poor. Poor but proud. But
perhaps soon, Mama dear, perhaps soon, not poor any
more—

"Jim and I are to pick out my ring this afternoon,

Mama!" I said. "The wedding date is set for Tuesday week. Just think, Mama darling—your little shabbily frocked girl is going to be Mrs. James Studdiford!"

Young Dr. Jim Studdiford, scion of Bay society, brilliant young surgeon, adored me—yes, me, hard-working shabby little Julia Page who wore well-mended gloves and well-darned stockings and carried fresh donuts home from the bakery at dusk for her widowed mama's supper!

"And are you happy about Jim, darling?" Mama asked me tenderly. "You *say* you are happy but sometimes a strange expression flits across your face—you seem worried over something."

Worried! I could laugh aloud in dear Mama's face! I am terrified. I have a secret gnawing at my heart, a secret so sinister that I must this very evening reveal it to Jim. I can bear it no longer. I must tell Jim that there will be no engagement ring, no wedding, no honeymoon trip on the great transatlantic steamer.

My secret is that I have a past. I slipped once, long ago, when I was barely sixteen, hardly more than a child, but I slipped nevertheless.

Lucky for me I didn't end up in a cage in Hong Kong.

"—and that's why I can't marry you, Jim." We were at tea in the St. Francis Hotel at a secluded table behind the palms. My voice and manner were swept bare of passion, I was infinitely fatigued.

Jim—dear Jim, with his boyishly rumpled hair and his laughing Irish eyes and his capable surgeon's hands—gazed at me uncomprehendingly.

"I don't understand," he said.

"I'm trying to tell you, Jim," I said. "That is how I bought my wisdom."

"What do you mean?" Jim said uneasily.

"*That,*" I said simply.*

Jim stood up. "I don't believe you," he said, with a short laugh.

"It's true," I said. "I was not yet sixteen. How long ago it seems! What I would not have given over these years to have blotted out that ugly stain!"

(Mrs. Norris was one terrific writer. To this day I think she is a terrific writer and I'm not ashamed to say so. I only wish I could write half as well as she did, so there.)

"Nobody has ever known but you, Jim," I said, "and although it is killing me and although I know this is the end for us, I am glad I told you."

"She's acting peculiar again," Grandfathah told Mother. "It's a different type peculiar from the old peculiar but still it's peculiar. For the sake of the family I advise you to have her treated by some competent physician."

"She sighs all the time," Joyce chimed in. "She walks around and sighs like this—'Aaagghh.'"

"I'm glad my big sister Cookie doesn't act crazy like your big sister does," obnoxious little Odette O'Gorsky said to Joyce.

"Leave Irene alone," my mother told everybody. "It's a phase she's going through. She'll get over it eventually."

I got over it. Eventually.

Before I got over it I went through several other periods, all of them mercifully brief, of being the heroine of something or other. I was Jo of *Little Women*—fun-loving hard-working red-knuckled shabby Jo—but it was too difficult having to cope with my sisters Meg, Beth, and Amy, all of whom had to be incorporated into my actual little sister Joyce, who refused flatly to co-operate in any way.

Marmee Trepel also turned stubborn and forbade me to

---

* See Chapter entitled "Love and Sex and All That Nonsense."

go up to our attic in order to scribble my stories the way Jo used to do.

"It's freezing up there," Marmee told me. "You'll stay down here in this nice warm living room like a civilized person, if you don't mind. And what do you think you're doing with that apple?"

Jo always took a rosy apple up to the attic with her to munch on while she scribbled.

"I'm going to eat it," I told Marmee sullenly.

"It's bad for your braces," Marmee said. "Eat a nice soft tangerine instead."

After I got over being Jo I was Patty of *When Patty Went to College*. At Patty's college the girls stirred a lot of homemade fudge in chafing dishes, but there were no chafing dishes in our kitchen in Brooklyn, besides which I wasn't allowed to eat fudge either because of the braces on my teeth, besides which I was only in my freshman year in Abraham Lincoln High School, so I gave up being Patty almost immediately.

For a few weeks after that I was a Julia once more—the violet-eyed raven-haired piquant heroine of Booth Tarkington's *Gentle Julia*—but since that Julia, I have been nobody. I have been just me.

Unless it turns out to be a particularly bad day around the house in which case I drop everything and mash my shabby velvet hat on my golden curls.

"Leave the dishes until I get back, Mama darling," I call. "I'm meeting Dr. Jim at the St. Francis for tea."

Of course if the cable cars don't happen to be running that day I simply stay at home riding Tarbaby around the plantation. It makes Grandfathah happy, po' soul.

# 15

# The End

When Mother died late in August she was in the midst of making a batch of Miss Parker's Tomato Soup and watching *The Secret Storm* and knitting a sweater for somebody in Appalachia and smoking her twenty-fifth cigarette of the day and drinking her tenth cup of coffee and working on a hooked rug and heaven knows what else.

"If anything happens to me," Mother used to say to Joyce and me, "promise that you'll find the cats a good home. Promise that you'll keep them together. Their little hearts would break if they were separated."

Has anybody out there ever tried to find a good home for two middle-aged cats, one Siamese, the other only part-Siamese, the poor darling?

"I love your mother so much," everybody told us. "I wonder if I could ask you two girls for some souvenir to remember her by. Something that belonged to her. Any little thing."

"Yes, indeed," Joyce and I replied promptly. "You can have her two cats."

"I was thinking more along the lines of one of her souvenir spoons," everybody said.

"You can have a souvenir spoon too," Joyce and I said. "You can have a souvenir spoon and the two cats."

"I'm afraid I can't possibly take the cats," everybody said. Joyce and I asked why everybody couldn't take the cats. "Small apartment," everybody said. "Also the baby and the sneezing and the fur and the allergist. Also the jealous dog."

At long last a wonderful person named Alfred Zega—a friend of Mother's—found the cats a home. Nellie and Prince Coronet Hudibras Gloriole now live together on a beautiful estate near Bridgewater, Connecticut, where they are allowed to eat all the freshly boiled shrimp and baby food that their little hearts desire.

Blessings on you, wonderful Alfred Zega! May the bluebird of happiness perch on your cuff links forever!

After Daddy died, Joyce and I had tried to talk Mother into selling the house and moving closer to town. The place was too isolated for her, we said. It was unsafe for a woman alone.

"Don't be silly," Mother pooh-poohed us. "Who would bother to come up a lonely road through the woods to hurt a woman like me?"

Her daughters refrained from replying, "Murderers, stranglers, hatchet killers, arsonists, rapists, and run-of-the-mill robbers, Mother dear."

Instead we said, "At least get yourself a good watchdog."

"Nellie's heart would break if I brought a dog into this house," Mother said. "The poor darling."

Mother lived on happily alone in the house for many

years. She was right, as usual. Nobody bothered to come up that lonely road through the woods to hurt her.

Only death.

The services were simple. Joyce and I asked Cyril if he would say a few words at the end. "Of course," Cyril said.

He spoke about what a warm and loving friend Mary had been to him, and to us all, and about how much all of us would miss her.

"And now I say good-bye to her," Cyril ended, sadly. "This is the first day since the day we met so long ago, dear Mary, that you have failed to interrupt me while I was speaking."